EXPLOITS OF DON QUIXOTE

Exploits of

DON QUIXOTE

Retold by James Reeves
Illustrated by Edward Ardizzone

BLACKIE: LONDON AND GLASGOW

ISBN 0 216 90467 6 (cased)
ISBN 0 216 90466 8 (paperback)

Blackie & Son Limited
Bishopbriggs, Glasgow G64 2NZ
450/452 Edgware Road, London W2 1EG

Printed in Great Britain by
Robert MacLehose and Company Limited
Printers to the University of Glasgow

CONTENTS

TO
SUSANNAH, QUENTIN AND DOMINIC
CLEMENCE
AND
JOANNA AND SARAH
ARDIZZONE

INTRODUCTION

The Spanish writer, Miguel de Cervantes, was born in 1547 and died in 1616, the same year as Shakespeare. He is said to have fought for the Holy Roman Empire against the Turks at the great sea battle of Lepanto in 1571. He later fell into the hands of Barbary pirates, and for some years was held a prisoner in Algiers. The rest of his life was spent in trying to earn a living by writing plays and novels. His greatest book, *Don Quixote*, was published in 1605, the second part in 1615. It tells of a poor gentleman who tries to re-live the heroic days of old by going in search of adventures in the manner of a knight errant of medieval romance.

For over three centuries readers in all countries have been delighted by the adventures of this absurd gentleman and his squire Sancho Panza. The reason for Quixote's popularity cannot be merely that he is ridiculous, or that he makes a nuisance of himself and gets into trouble wherever he goes. Quixote is the embodiment, even though he is also the exaggeration, of a great idea. This idea is that there is more in life than the humdrum routine of everyday affairs; that true greatness is to be found only in the spirit of service to an ideal. That the ideal is, with Quixote, only an illusion does not detract from its fascination, though it does make him a pathetic figure. To attempt the impossible for the sake of honour—to add to the store of human greatness by risking everything without the hope of material reward—to endure danger and hardship because endurance itself is noble: this is the quixotic ideal, and the world would be the poorer without it. That is the secret of Don Quixote's universal appeal. We may, indeed we must, laugh at his absurdity; yet if there is anything of chivalry or generosity in us, we cannot help being on his side, however innocent his victims. We know he cannot win, but his misguided valour excites our pity with our laughter.

Sancho Panza, the simple yet shrewd squire, the lover of creature-comforts and material well-being, is the perfect foil to his master. Sancho is the ordinary man, sometimes brave but more often a coward, the embodiment of all the peasant virtues. Without him, life could hardly go on. Yet when the call of adventure comes, he is not deaf to it; when the vision of a greatness beyond himself appears dimly before his eyes, he is not blind. He gets very little from his service to Quixote except hard knocks and disappointed hopes; but his loyalty is its own reward. No one can doubt that his life has been illuminated and enriched by his association with his master.

Knight and squire represent two sides of human nature—the desire to lead and the desire to serve; the need for a spiritual aim and the need for material well-being; the balance between madness and common sense, illusion and reality, courage and prudence. Cervantes, in creating these two complementary figures, not only invented a tale of lasting charm, pathos and humour, he made a unique contribution to humanity's knowledge of itself.

In its entirety the book is of enormous length and contains much that is tedious to modern minds and quite beyond the grasp of young readers. Yet it has been felt, like many of the old romances which were never intended for children, to be in essence a classic for the young. It is right that children should be introduced to the quixotic idea, even if they cannot enjoy all of the knight's adventures and the lengthy digressions with which they are spun out. I have here made a new selection of these exploits which appeal most readily to younger readers; in doing so, I have had to abridge and re-write somewhat freely. Yet I hope that my adaptation is in the spirit of the original and introduces nothing which is alien to it.

J. R.

Chalfont St. Giles
1959

— 1 —

Don Quixote in Search of Adventure

There was once a country gentleman living in Spain in a region they call la Mancha. He was perhaps fifty years old, but he looked older. His form was tall but thin; his eyes were bright, but his cheeks were sunken, as if from much care and thought; his head was grizzled and unkempt. Yet his beard, and the grave tones of his voice, gave him an air of dignity, so that you would have known him anywhere as a gentleman of good breeding and ancient family.

His house and his estate were in bad repair. The plaster on the walls was cracked, and the doors grated on their hinges. His garden was neglected, for he had only one manservant to act as butler, groom and gardener.

The rest of his household consisted of his niece and an old housekeeper. Like many country gentlemen of his time, he kept a lance and a buckler hanging on the wall, and in his stable a horse and a greyhound, for he had once spent much time in hunting. He lived very poorly on such things as mutton broth and lentils, and on Sundays perhaps a pigeon or some other little delicacy.

Poor gentleman, he did not go hunting now! He scarcely ever trotted out with his greyhound at his heels, in the fresh morning air. He had, alas! only one interest in life—his old, musty books. How his housekeeper grumbled as she lifted the great leather-bound volumes and put them in piles to make his study tidy! How his niece sighed if she found him deep in one of his books when she wanted to talk to him! Rows and rows of them he had—shelves full and tables full, and still he bought more. He even sold part of his land to buy books. And what were they all about?

They were nothing but great long stories of the days of old—stories of knights in armour and fair ladies in distress, of giants and ogres, witches and fairies, battles, quests, and all manner of marvels and wonders. He had ten whole volumes about King Arthur, Queen Guinevere, Sir Lancelot and the Knights of the Round Table. He had at least as many dealing with King Charlemagne and his peers—of whom Roland was the most illustrious. Quixote had also a number of precious books describing the spells and enchantments by which wizards turned themselves into hideous monsters and got power over the helpless youths and maidens; and he had other books giving accounts of all the famous castles of old—in Turkey, in Spain, in Britain, France and Germany.

The gentleman spent his days and nights in the study of such things. Passers-by grew used to seeing the lamp in his window burn late as he turned over the yellow pages. He read far into the morning; or if he began reading in the day time, then he went on far into the night. When he had finished reading some old tale or other, he would hunt out the parson or the barber to argue with him as to whether Arthur or Roland was the greater knight, or to tell some discovery he had made about a damsel locked in a dark tower. The days of such heroes and ladies were long past, but the gentleman of la Mancha dreamed of bringing them back. He grew haggard from want of sleep and thin from want of food. In time the villagers believed he had lost his wits, for he could think and talk of nothing but enchantments; indeed his head was stuffed so full of fables that not only was there no room for ordinary, everyday matters, but he began to think the world was just as it had been in days gone by.

At last he rose one day from reading a great parchment book, and made a solemn resolution.

'I will be,' he said, 'a knight errant. The world is full of adventures, but there is none to follow them. I will go forth and see what wrongs there are to be righted. I will fight against giants! I will rescue maidens in distress! I will free princes who have been changed by foul witches into toads and serpents! There are great deeds to be done, and I will do them!'

So saying, he went to a storehouse in a corner of the yard, and there he found a suit of rusty armour that had belonged to his grandfather. He took a scrubbing brush and began to scour it clean. After many laborious hours he succeeded in removing some of the rust. It was not perhaps the sort of armour that Sir Lancelot of the Lake would have worn, but it was better than nothing. Next he scraped and burnished a rusty sword with the blade all hacked and hewn. Then he turned his attention to the

19

helmet. Alas, the visor—that is, the face-piece—was quite gone; so he took cardboard and string and made a new one. To test its strength, he slashed at it with the sword. In less than twenty seconds a whole week's work was cut to pieces!

'Well, that wouldn't have been much use,' he said cheerfully, and set to work to make another. At last it was finished. More prudently, he did not test it this time, but fastened it on to the head-piece with green ribbon, and so made what he thought was a very passable helmet for a knight errant.

'Now for a horse!' he said. 'What great hero was ever without his trusty steed? Alexander the Great had his Bucephalus: I shall have—what?'

Now he had no horse in his stable except the old bony nag that had served as a hunter in better days, and was now only used on occasions to carry the manservant to the town. It was all skin and bones and scarcely fit for service at all. It had a downcast and sorrowful air which came from feeding on thin grass and trying in vain to remember the flavour of good oats.

'What shall I name you, old creature?' the gentleman wondered. But the nag only snuffled and pawed the stableyard feebly. At last he hit on the splendid and high-sounding name of 'Rosinante', which is a Spanish word meaning something like 'Nag-of-All-Nags'. And this the gentleman thought a most suitable name for a knight errant's faithful charger.

Next he began to consider a title for himself. This took him a full eight days. He searched his books, he puzzled his brain, and in due time, after much hesitation, he settled upon the name of 'Don Quixote of la Mancha'. For la Mancha, you remember, was the region where he livcd, and he thought by thus honouring his native country to add glory and fame to its history.

'And now,' said Don Quixote to himself, 'there is one thing more—and that the most important of all. I have armour, I have a horse, I have a great and noble name; but I have no lady. What is a knight without a lady? For whose sake shall I perform the gallant deeds I mean to do? To whose feet shall I carry the giant I mean to capture, so that he may say to her, as they do in the books: "Fair madam, I am the giant So-and-so, vanquished in mortal combat by the illustrious and never-to-be-sufficiently-extolled Cavalier, Don Quixote of la Mancha, come hither to lay my unworthy carcass before you, that you may dispose of me according to your will"?'

Poor Quixote knew of no lady worthy to receive the submission of the giant So-and-so. At last he remembered a young woman who lived in a near-by town, milking the cows and working in the fields. It was she who would have to be his lady; it was she for whom he would suffer hardship and fight battles. She too must have a name worthy of the deeds he meant to do in her honour, for her own namc, which was no more high-sounding than our English 'Sally', would scarcely do. Once more the gentleman creased his high forehead in thought, and in the end he decided to call his lady 'Dulcinea of Toboso'. The name 'Dulcinea' suggested everything that was gentle and gracious, while 'Toboso' was the town where she lived.

All was now ready. One fine spring morning, when the dew was still on the bushes and the larks were carolling overhead, Don Quixote, without saying a word to anyone, fastened on his ancient armour as best he could, took up his sword and shield, and clattered out to the stable-yard. There he coaxed the unwilling Rosinanate

21

from his stall and strapped a saddle of frayed leather upon his back. Climbing stiffly astride, he turned the horse's head and set off on his adventures. As the old nag stumbled forth, blinking sleepily in the morning sun, these words came to Don Quixote's lips:

'For thy sake, O gentle lady Dulcinea of Toboso, may a blessing light upon the exploits of the renowned and peerless Don Quixote of la Mancha!'

But even if the lady herself had been present at that time, she would not have heard his words for no sound could have passed through the cardboard visor which covered the gentleman's face.

— 2 —

Don Quixote Knighted

As Don Quixote rode along, dreaming of the wonderful adventures he was going to have, a thought struck him which was so fearful that he almost turned back and went home. He had not yet been made a knight! Now according to the rules of chivalry, no man who has not been knighted has the right to fight with other knights and kill them. So poor Don Quixote would not be able to perform the valiant deeds he meant to do. For how could he show his great skill, or rescue maidens in distress, if he was not allowed to kill other brave knights?

'Well,' he said to himself, 'I will ride on, and perhaps I shall meet someone who can make me a knight. Of course I ought to have white armour too, with no coat of arms upon it. But perhaps if I can scrub a little more of the rust off this old armour of mine, it will pass for white.'

So all day he rode across the empty plain with Rosinante struggling patiently along beneath him. The day became very hot. Horse and rider grew weary and faint with hunger and thirst. Not a soul came in sight. Quixote let Rosinante carry him where he would, and all the time he talked to himself about the glories of knight errantry.

At last, towards nightfall, he came to an inn. Outside it stood two country girls on their way to Seville, chatting to each other.

'Aha!' said he to himself. 'This is some nobleman's castle, and these ladies have strolled out to take the evening air.'

And indeed the inn, poor and humble though it was, did appear to his eyes like a great fortress with turrets and battlements, upon which he supposed that a dwarf would presently appear, blow his horn, and announce the arrival of a wandering knight.

It so happened that just as Quixote rode up to the inn, a swineherd not far off blew a blast on his horn to call his pigs together for the night.

'Splendid!' thought Quixote. 'My coming has been announced.'

But the two country girls were terrified at the appearance of the rider in ancient armour on the bony nag. They had never seen anyone like this before.

'Fly not, gentle maidens!' cried Quixote. 'I am but a wandering knight come in search of the lord of this fair castle.'

At this the girls laughed aloud, and just then the innkeeper came out. He was a fat, comfortable-looking fellow in a coarse apron, but to Quixote he appeared like the governor of the fortress.

'Sir Governor,' said Quixote, 'I desire to lodge this

night under your noble roof and to partake of your hospitality.'

The innkeeper was surprised to be spoken to in this way, but he supposed that his guest's mind had been affected by the heat of the day, so he told him that he might spend the night there and take rest and refreshment.

'See that my steed is well cared for,' added Quixote, 'for, as you see, he is a noble beast and is to bear me on my journey in search of knightly deeds.'

The innkeeper was more surprised than ever, for he had seldom seen a more miserable-looking hack than poor Rosinante, who, for want of rest and food, was almost dropping to the ground.

Don Quixote and the innkeeper went inside, and the two country girls followed, to see the fun. It was a Friday, so the only food that could be provided was fish—some dried-up salt cod and stale black bread. Now Quixote's visor had been tied on with green ribbons, and he asked the girls to untie them. But this they couldn't do, and as Quixote refused to have them cut, he was forced to eat with his visor on. So one of the girls held up the visor while Quixote fed himself. As for wine, he could in no way drink it from a glass, so the innkeeper pushed a hollow reed through his helmet and poured the wine through it. Certainly, no one had ever had such a strange meal in that inn before!

Just then a sow-doctor blew on his pipe of reeds to announce his arrival at the inn. To Don Quixote this sounded like rare music.

'Ah,' thought he, 'this is a great and famous castle, and there are musicians to play while the company banquets. What delicate food this is—fresh river trout and good white bread!'

Suddenly, however, Quixote remembered that he was not yet a knight. Until he was, he couldn't take part in any glorious adventures. So he sprang up from the table and led the innkeeper outside. He took him to the stable and, after shutting the door, he fell on his knees at the astonished innkeeper's feet.

'Sir Knight,' he cried, 'and Governor of this castle, I swear that I will never rise from this position until you promise to grant me a boon.'

'Now come, sir,' said the innkeeper. 'Stand up! There's no need to go down on your knees to me.'

'Nay, sir,' went on Quixote earnestly, 'I have sworn that I will never rise until you grant my request.'

The innkeeper, who was now quite certain that his guest was mad, thought he had better do as he was asked.

'Very well, sir,' he said, 'what is the boon you ask? If it's within my power, I'll do it, and gladly.'

'My Lord Governor,' answered Quixote, 'tomorrow morning early I desire that you admit me to the order of knighthood. All this night I will watch over my armour, and in the morning you will touch me upon my neck and shoulders with my sword and make me a knight. Then I shall be allowed to perform the deeds of valour which I burn to do!'

'So that's it,' said the innkeeper. 'Very well, sir, I'll do as you ask.'

'Come then,' said Quixote, rising. 'Lead me to the chapel, that I may begin my watch.'

'As to that,' said the innkeeper, 'I—er—I'm afraid the chapel was burnt to the ground a while back, and—er—hasn't yet been rebuilt. But you may watch just as well in the courtyard, and in the morning I'll make you a knight.'

So Don Quixote took off his armour and laid it carefully across a water-trough that stood beside the pump in the yard. Then he began to pace to and fro, muttering a prayer that he might be a worthy member of the order of knighthood to which he was soon to belong.

The moon shone as brightly as if it were daylight, and the guests at the inn could clearly see Don Quixote's extraordinary behaviour. Soon quite a crowd of people had gathered at the far end of the yard, hardly able to keep from laughing out loud.

Presently a carrier arrived, and stopped his wagon in the yard to water his horse. He was just going to lift the armour from the water-trough when Quixote told him angrily to leave it alone.

'O miserable slave!' he cried. 'Know you not that the arms you seek to move are those of the most illustrious warrior that ever carried sword? Get back this instant, and touch not these sacred things!'

The carrier took not the slightest heed, and seizing Quixote's armour by the straps, pitched it across the yard.

Don Quixote raised his eyes to the moon and said, 'O peerless Dulcinea, goddess and guide of my life, give me strength to put an end to the wretched varlet who dares to touch with his unworthy hand the arms of your sworn defender!'

Not understanding a word of this nonsense, the carrier laughed aloud, and Don Quixote, seizing his lance in both hands, gave him such a blow that he fell groaning to the earth. Quixote then replaced his lance and the rest of his armour across the water-trough and began once more to pace to and fro, calling upon his lady to reward him for his bravery.

Just then a second carrier came with a bucket to get

27

water for his horse, and he too picked up the armour that lay across the trough and pitched it roughly aside.

Once more Quixote grasped his lance and, roaring terribly, knocked the second carrier to the ground as he had done the first. This was too much for the onlookers, among whom were some of the carrier's friends. Some of them laughed, others jeered, while some began to abuse Quixote and throw stones at him.

Quixote, not in the least discouraged, cried out:

'O beauteous lady Dulcinea, hear my prayer and come to my aid in crushing these worthless wretches who thus molest your true and faithful servant. As for you, you vile and beastly crowd, get away from here, and cease to trouble the great and illustrious Don Quixote of la Mancha, who is even now watching over his magnificent and never-to-be-dishonoured arms!'

This was uttered with such fury and deadly earnestness that the onlookers shrank away in terror, and the inn-keeper, fearing that there might be a brawl, begged them to go away and leave the mad gentleman alone. So the wounded carriers were helped to their feet, and Quixote was left alone with the innkeeper.

'Come, sir,' said the innkeeper, 'you've watched long enough if you ask me, and I don't see why you shouldn't be knighted right away. So let's get it over and done with.'

So saying, he made Quixote kneel before him once more. Then he took hold of his account book, for he had no Bible, opened it and began to mumble any nonsense that came into his head. Next, he took Quixote's rusty sword and gave him a couple of smart blows, one on the neck and the other on the shoulders.

'Arise, Sir Knight,' he pronounced in a solemn voice, and Quixote arose stiffly to his feet. The inkeeper handed

the knight's sword to one of the two country girls, and
his spurs to the other. The girls solemnly strapped them
on to Quixote, hardly able to do up the buckles for
laughing. Never, thought they, had they seen such a
ridiculous pantomime in all their lives!

'I thank you,' said Don Quixote gravely to the girl
who had given him his sword. 'And who may you be?'

She told him she was a cobbler's daughter from
Toledo.

'Henceforward,' said Quixote, 'be a lady—one of the
proudest and most noble in all Spain.'

The girl curtsied and turned away to hide her amusement.

Then Quixote asked the other who she was, and she
told him she was a miller's daughter, and Quixote bowed
gravely to her, thanked her for his spurs, and told her

too to think of herself as a great and noble lady.

Then he saddled Rosinante, and bade farewell to the innkeeper.

'I thank you, illustrious governor of this renowned fortress, for the magnificence of your entertainment, and for the unspeakable honour you have done in conferring on me the order of knighthood—an order I shall in all things endeavour not to disgrace.'

The innkeeper was overcome with mirth at his guest's astonishing behaviour, and at the same time so relieved that the adventure had ended without serious mishap, that he did not hand Quixote a bill for his lodging. Instead, he held his stirrup for him, helped him on to his horse, and wished him God-speed.

Don Quixote grasped his lance and his shield, gave a tug at Rosinante's reins, wished everyone good-bye once more, and rode out of the inn yard in search of more adventures.

Dawn was breaking on the far horizon, and the two girls and the innkeeper watched the tall, gaunt figure on the ramshackle nag disappear unsteadily in the distance.

Never before in all their lives, they told each other, had they passed a merrier night. It was not often that such a comical traveller came to the humble inn.

— 3 —

The Adventure of the Silk Merchants

Don Quixote rode along with joy in his heart because he had been made a knight and so was the equal of the other proud and bold knights he would meet on the road. The sun shone and the birds chirruped in the blue sky.

'O Dulcinea,' cried Quixote, 'light of my soul and moon of my firmament! How fortunate you are to have such a brave and enterprising knight to defend your name and sing your praises! Ah, if only you were here to receive my homage and to reward my devotion with a smile for your gracious and never-to-be-sufficiently-admired countenance! Now where shall I go in search of noble exploits to perform in your name and for your service?'

He came to a cross-roads, and there he decided, as other wandering knights had done before him, to let his horse have his head. So saying, he let the reins drop from his hand as a sign to Rosinante that he might go the way he wished. Rosinante at once took the road to la Mancha, for the one wish in his heart was to see the inside of his stable again. So for a while horse and rider jogged along the homeward road.

Soon Don Quixote distinguished a cloud of white dust in the distance, and a few minutes later he saw that it was caused by a party of riders coming towards him.

'Aha!' said he. 'Here are some knights, riding out like myself in search of adventure. No doubt they will wish to acknowledge the beauty and wisdom of the faultless Dulcinea.'

When the party reached him, he saw that there were six well-clad gentlemen, four servants, and three muleteers. The gentlemen were in fact merchants from Toledo, who were on their way to Murcia to buy silks, but Quixote did not know this. Indeed, even if he had known it, he would still have thought they were knights errant. So he made Rosinante halt in the very middle of the road, drew his lance, brandished his shield, and roared forth in a loud and commanding voice:

'Ho, knights! Stand, and attend! Before I let you pass, I demand that you pay homage to my lady, the peerless Dulcinea of Toboso, acknowledging that of all ladies in Spain she is the most gracious, the most beauteous, and the most renowned!'

Astonished by this speech, the merchants and their servants stood still and gazed at the gaunt figure in rusty armour astride the bony hack. Some of them began to laugh, and to murmur to each other that they had met a lunatic; but one of the merchants, who was something of a joker, stepped forward and addressed Quixote thus, pretending to take him seriously:

'Sir Knight,' said he, 'we will readily acknowledge your lady to be the fairest in all Spain—nay, in the whole world if necessary—but how can we do so without having set eyes on her? Now if your honour will be so kind as to bring forth the lady that we may look at her, I am sure we will all instantly bow down at her feet and do homage to her loveliness as you desire.'

'That will I not do!' said Quixote stoutly. 'For if I show you the lady, what is the use of your acclaiming her beauty, which will then be obvious to all eyes? No, proud knight, what I demand is that you shall acknowledge her beauty *without* having seen her! Anybody can admit that a lady he has seen is beautiful. But to admit the beauty of one whom he has *not* seen—that is the act of a true knight, an act of faith!'

'Why, sir,' said the merchant, 'only show us her portrait—even a tiny portrait. Even if the lady was squint-eyed and had no teeth, we would, out of courtesy, be ready to proclaim her beauty. But it would be a load on our conscience, the conscience of Christian gentlemen, to swear to the beauty of someone we had not seen!'

'The lady is *not* squint-eyed,' shouted Quixote indignantly, 'nor is she toothless. How dare you make so infamous a suggestion? I will not insult her person by showing her picture to such as you! Either admit to her beauty without having seen her, or be prepared for the fate that will befall you.'

The merchants stubbornly refused Quixote's demand, so that the knight called out:

'Very well, cowardly and base wretches, so you defy the commands of the illustrious Don Quixote of la Mancha! So be it—and have at you!'

With these words, he grasped his shield and lance

34

with more determination than ever, and set spurs to the meagre sides of poor Rosinante. The horse shot forward, but caught one of his hooves on a loose stone, tripped over and sprawled in the road. Quixote's lance and shield fell from his grasp, and he tried to get to his feet. But his armour prevented him, so that he was forced to sit in the dust of the road, raising his fist in anger and shaking it at the merchants and their servants, who were now overcome with laughter.

'Fly not!' cried Quixote. 'You have been saved, not by your own valour but by the clumsiness of my horse. Only wait till I can get to my feet, and I will gladly take you on, singly or all together, for the honour of knighthood and for the fame of the renowned Dulcinea of Toboso.'

By this time the merchants and the rest of the party

had lost patience with the knight, and one of the mule-teers, seeing that Quixote was now unarmed and quite harmless, picked up his lance and began beating him soundly. Upon poor Quixote's back he rained blow after blow until the lance was broken into splinters. Then the silk merchants, their servants and muleteers continued on their way, leaving Quixote still sprawling and helpless in the road. When the laughter of the departing merchants had died away in the distance, Quixote began to bewail his unhappy fate, reciting one of the sorrowful ballads he had learned from his books about knighthood.

At last a labourer from his own village of la Mancha, returning home with his ass, came upon the extraordinary figure of the knight in armour, sitting in the road reciting poetry in pitiful tones—though he could scarcely hear what Quixote said because of the cardboard visor which covered his mouth.

'Now who can this be?' said the labourer, stopping beside him. 'It is some poor gentleman who is out of his wits and is in need of help.'

What was his surprise, then, on removing the battered visor, to behold the dusty visage of his well-known and ever-respected neighbour.

'Why, Master Quixote!' cried he. 'Whatever are you doing here in this state?'

Without listening to Quixote's rambling tale of bad knights and fair ladies, he helped him to his feet, brushed away some of the dust with which he was covered, and helped him on to his own ass. For he thought Quixote would be safer there than on Rosinante. And so, leading the ass with one hand and Rosinante with the other, he brought Don Quixote back to la Mancha. He waited till it was night, for he did not want to bring such a ridiculous figure into his native village in daylight, for everyone to gaze at and make fun of.

Now it so happened that at the moment when Quixote reached his own house, a scene of confusion and dismay was taking place inside. For the housekeeper, alarmed at her master's long absence, had called in the priest and the barber, both good friends of Quixote's, to decide what should be done.

'Depend upon it,' said the housekeeper, 'it is those wicked books that have done all this mischief. If I had my way, I'd burn the lot for the wickedness they've caused in leading my poor master out of his mind.'

'Yes, indeed,' said Don Quixote's niece. 'Many's the time he has stayed up all night reading and reciting from his books, and when I've come into the library in the morning I've found him jumping up and down, slashing at the wall with his sword until it's all battered into holes!'

'Why does he do that?' asked the priest.

'He supposes he's fighting with giants,' answered the niece.

'Yes,' said the housekeeper, 'and those same giants have come out of these wicked books, and nowhere else.'

'Perhaps, then,' said the barber, 'we should be doing your master a service if we were to take his books away. There's a strange power in books, it seems, to lead a man astray. But where can he be, I wonder?'

Just then, as if in answer to his words, the sound of a furious knocking was heard on the outer door.

'In the name of chivalry,' called out the voice of Quixote in resolute and commanding tones, 'open up and admit the noble and right valiant Don Quixote, foremost among knights and equal to the twelve peers

of France and the nine worthies of the ancient world!'

'All right, all right!' cried the barber. 'Coming—coming!'

With that he opened the door and admitted the battered and dusty knight, led by the kind labourer who had rescued him on the road.

The labourer was thanked for his pains, and the housekeeper and the niece helped Quixote off with his armour.

'All I need,' said Quixote, 'is rest and food. Get me something to eat, good woman, and let me go to bed to repose my weary limbs after my adventures and hardships.'

So Quixote went off to bed, and when she had seen to his needs the housekeeper went to the library to help the priest and the barber carry his books out to the courtyard.

In the morning, before Quixote was awake, a great bonfire was made on the stones, and all those mischievous books of knighthood and romance were burnt to ashes. Some few, which were less harmful than the rest, and which were thought to be valuable, were saved; but the greater part of them went up in flames, never again to be read by the eyes of man. Thus did Quixote's friends think they had cured him of his madness.

— 4 —

Sancho Panza, the Windmills, and Other Matters

While Quixote lay in bed, dreaming of knights and giants, and sometimes calling out in his sleep, the priest and the barber consulted with the housekeeper as to what was best to be done next. They decided to get a man to wall up the room in which the books had been kept, so that the cause of all the trouble might be entirely forgotten.

'We must tell him,' said the barber, 'that the devil came in the night and took away his books, and even the library itself.'

'Better still,' said Quixote's niece, 'if we say it was some enchanter who was his special enemy. He will believe that, for certain.'

This was done. A mason was called in hurriedly to take away the door of the library and put a wall in its place. When Quixote woke up, he demanded first food and then his books.

'What books?' asked the housekeeper. 'There are no such things here, sir.'

'Why, uncle,' said his niece, 'a terrible enchanter, whose name I do not know, came here last night and filled the house with smoke. Then he must have carried away your books, together with the library itself, for there is no sign of them.'

Quixote, after searching the house, said it must have been as they had told him, and he swore there and then to be revenged upon his enemy, the terrible enchanter who had come in the night and stolen his library.

During the next few days the priest tried to argue with Quixote and persuade him to give up looking for adventures and stay at home in the care of his kind housekeeper and his niece. But Quixote had formed another plan.

He went down to the village and talked to a poor labouring man called Sancho Panza, who was a simple, foolish fellow with a wife and several children.

'Friend Sancho,' said the knight, 'I have need of a squire to go with me on my travels, to share my adventures and see to my needs. Will you go with me?'

Sancho Panza said he did not know how he could leave his family.

'If you come with me,' said Quixote, 'you shall have fame and glory. All the great knights of the past had their squires, and in the end they rewarded them for their faithful service. Now I shall be sure of winning lands and wealth, and I shall make you governor of some island. How would you like that? You shall be king, and your wife queen, and your children princes and princesses.'

'As to that, sir,' answered Sancho, 'I'm not sure that my old woman would make much of a queen. Still, I wouldn't half like to have an island of my own to be king

41

of. So if your honour can promise me this, I'll go along with you, and gladly.'

'Splendid!' cried Quixote. 'We will set out at once. I will ride upon my fine stallion Rosinante, and you shall run by my side.'

'As to that, your honour,' said Sancho, 'I'm no great hand at running. I'm not as slender as I was, and I've got a good-tempered donkey called Dapple who'll carry me a sight better than my own two legs.'

Don Quixote was not at all sure that the brave knights of old would have allowed their squires to ride donkeys. Still, he gave in and said:

'Very well, friend Sancho, I will permit you to ride your ass, until such time as I shall unhorse some wandering knight and present you with his steed.'

So it was arranged. Quixote went home to repair his armour as best he might, while Sancho provided himself with a pair of saddle-bags to carry provisions and spare clothes. With these he loaded Dapple together with a fat leather bottle full of good red wine, for he had no intention of travelling without refreshment. Next day, without taking any leave of their families, knight and squire set off together across the plain in search of daring exploits.

They had not been riding long before there appeared on the far horizon thirty or forty great windmills.

'Aha!' cried Quixote, his eyes gleaming with the light of adventure. 'Come, friend Sancho, and assist me while I do battle against yonder army of great and mighty giants!'

'What giants, your worship?' asked Sancho.

Just then a gust of wind blew across the plain, and the sails of the windmills began to turn.

'See yonder,' said Quixote. 'There must be over thirty of them, and they are waving their mighty arms as if to defy us. I will charge against them single-handed. If you won't come with me, stay here and pray for my success; and you shall see what a splendid and chivalrous act I shall perform against this redoubtable army.'

Sancho was certain there were no giants, but he could see that it was useless to argue; for his master had already clapped spurs to Rosinante's sides and was preparing to charge against the windmills.

'Fly not, false cowards!' shouted Quixote, his lance quivering before him as he rode nearer and nearer. 'Perhaps you are the foul enchanters who stole my books! Now I shall have revenge upon you, not only for that theft, but for all the other base and treacherous deeds that you have performed against the people of this country.'

Then he called upon the peerless Dulcinea to aid him in his single-handed onslaught, and urged Rosinante to a gallop. His lance pierced one of the revolving sails of the nearest windmill, and both he and his horse were dragged violently towards it. Then the lance was shivered to fragments, and Don Quixote, thrown from his saddle, rolled headlong across the plain.

Sancho Panza trotted up to rescue his master.

'O my goodness,' he said, 'now look what you've gone and done! I knew it was no good your worship setting on a lot of harmless windmills. If I was you, sir——'

'Silence, friend!' said Quixote sternly. 'Let not a squire question the deeds of his brave master. For I can see things that are hidden from your eyes!'

'Indeed, that is so,' agreed Sancho. 'But your worship

scared me. Honest, you did, sir. I really can't see as how charging one of those things is going to get us anywhere.'

'Sancho,' said Quixote, preparing to remount Rosinante, 'it is the duty of every true knight to destroy utterly all giants, dragons and false enchanters. If he fail to do so, he is unworthy of the title of knight, and of the service of his lady.'

'Very good, sir,' said Sancho, 'just as you say. But now you've disposed of the giants, what about a bite of dinner?'

'Not yet,' said Quixote. 'We must go on.'

So they proceeded, Quixote on Rosinante and Sancho on Dapple, who was well trussed up with saddle-bags containing the food he so dearly wanted to get at.

After a while night began to fall, and Quixote said they might rest under an oak tree. They dismounted, and Sancho gladly pulled out some food from one of the bags, and began to help himself generously from his wine-bottle.

'Ah well,' he said to himself, 'it's not so bad, this wandering life—at least it's a change. And won't it be fun when I'm king of some island!'

But Quixote refused to eat. He seemed to have no interest in food and wine. Instead, he settled down to pass the night in thinking about his absent lady, the glorious Dulcinea of Toboso, for he had read that all true knights spend many sleepless hours in dreaming of their absent ladies. As for Sancho Panza, it was not long before he was sleeping soundly, and only his deep and comfortable snoring disturbed the silence of the night.

Next day they were up early, and it was not long before they were once more jogging across the plain. Soon a party of people were seen in the distance. When they came nearer, Quixote and his squire could make out two large figures in black seated upon enormous mules. They wore masks to keep the dust from their faces, and they carried sunshades over their heads. They were attended by several country lads. Behind them was a coach containing a lady and her companion on their way to Seville, escorted by four or five horsemen and several muleteers.

'Oho!' said Sancho to himself, as he saw his master looking eagerly towards the advancing party. 'More giants, I shouldn't wonder!'

Now the two men in black were no other than monks, but to Don Quixote they were enchanters who were carrying off some fair lady imprisoned in the coach. The monks had, indeed, nothing to do with the ladies in the coach, and were merely riding in the same direction for company.

'See you those wicked magicians?' Quixote asked Sancho. 'Look how your valiant master undertakes to free those innocent maidens whom they have captured and are even now on their way to shut up in the dungeon of their foul castle!'

'O have a care, master,' entreated Sancho. 'I'll swear these are nothing but a pair of simple monks and no magicians, as you say.'

'Shame upon you!' cried Quixote, standing boldly up in his stirrups in the middle of the road. 'Hold, foul enchanters!' he cried, as the monks approached. 'Deliver up yon unhappy princesses, or I shall wipe you from the face of the earth.'

'Sir,' said the foremost of the monks, 'I assure you we know nothing of any princesses. We do but go peaceably on our way, hurtful to no one.'

45

'You lie!' shouted Quixote, and without further speech he charged full at the unfortunate monk. The second monk, seeing what was going on, rode to one side as nimbly as he could; but the first monk could only avoid Quixote's weapon by prudently falling off his mule. Seeing his enemy thus easily vanquished, Quixote rode up to the coach to offer his compliments to the ladies, while Sancho dismounted beside the fallen monk and began to help himself to his clothes.

'Surely,' said he to himself, 'these are the spoils of battle. My master has beaten this fellow, and I am entitled to his possessions.'

But the monk's servants, seeing that the ferocious Don Quixote was not looking, stepped up to Sancho and began beating him soundly, having first knocked him to the ground in defence of their master. Then they helped the monk to his feet, and he very sensibly remounted his mule and rode off to join his friend, without waiting to see what happened next.

'Fair damsels,' said Quixote to the ladies in the coach, 'you are indeed fortunate in being delivered from these foul enchanters by the prowess of the thrice-famous and utterly resplendent flower of chivalry, Don Quixote of la Mancha. Know that it is he and no other who has rescued you from your doleful and ill-deserved plight. Ladies, I beg you, go now to Toboso and pay your humble respects to the peerless Dulcinea, who is the soul and guiding star of him who has saved you!'

'We shall do no such thing!' said one of the men escorting the ladies. 'Toboso is far out of our way. We're going to Seville, and if you'll kindly get out of the way, you meddlesome old idiot, we'll be on our road!'

This speech was too much for Quixote.

'If you were a gentleman,' said he, 'I should fight with you. As it is, slave, I command you to be silent and not interfere with what does not concern you.'

For answer the man raised his sword and gave Quixote such a blow that, had it not been for his armour, he would certainly have split him down to the waist. This so enraged the knight that he in turn felled him to the ground.

At this the ladies in the coach cried out in alarm, and begged Quixote to spare their unfortunate servant.

'This will I do, noble ladies,' answered Quixote gallantly, 'on one condition, as is required by the laws of chivalry. See that your unworthy follower goes instantly to Toboso and delivers himself up to the renowned Dulcinea, that she may do what she will with him.'

The ladies promised that it should be as he said. The

47

servant was then allowed to get to his feet, and the whole party set off along the road.

When they had gone, Sancho, who had now somewhat recovered from his beating, came up to Don Quixote and said:

'Now master, what about giving me that island? Surely it's time I was made a king.'

'Not yet, friend Sancho,' answered Quixote. 'There is much to be done before that can be. Meanwhile, let us remount our faithful steeds and proceed on our way.'

Sancho Panza shrugged his shoulders and, after a last long pull at his bottle, did as his master had bidden.

— 5 —
The Adventure of the Yanguesan Carriers

Don Quixote and Sancho rode on until they came to a fair green meadow, where they decided to rest during the heat of the day. They loosed Rosinante and Dapple and let them roam in the meadow, while master and man opened the saddle-bags and began to feed on the provisions that Sancho had brought.

Now it so happened that a party of carriers from Yangues, who were driving some mares along the road, had stopped in that valley to allow their cattle to graze in the long grass. Rosinante, catching sight of the mares, trotted across the meadow to talk to them; but they had no thought for Rosinante, only for the rich grass. So not wanting to be troubled by him, they attacked him with their hooves and teeth. The Yanguesan carriers ran up, in order to help their mares drive away Rosinante. They so beat the poor nag with their staves that his saddle

49

girths were broken, the saddle thrown from his back, and he himself rolled on the ground in pain. Quixote and his squire, seeing the plight that had befallen the knight's horse, ran across the field to his assistance, and as they ran Quixote called out:

'Friend Sancho, I see these men are no knights, but only a pack of rascals and fellows of low rank. I tell you this, so that you may lawfully help me to revenge the injury done to my noble steed before our very eyes. The rules of chivalry, though they forbid you to attack a knight, allow you to fight with low-born wretches such as these.'

'What's all this about revenge?' asked Sancho. 'Can't you see, sir, that there's about twenty of them and only two of us? That'll be a fine revenge!'

'I myself,' said Don Quixote proudly, 'am worth a hundred ordinary men. Why, Sancho, we may say that these fellows are outnumbered.'

Without further speech he drew his sword and charged upon the Yanguesans. Sancho stoutly followed his master's example and rushed towards the carriers. Quixote's first stroke cut through the leather jerkin of the carrier who happened to be nearest; whereupon his fellows, seeing that they were set upon by only two men, surrounded Quixote and Sancho, prepared to make mincemeat of them. Sancho was speedily knocked to the ground, and not long afterwards the knight was struck down and fell at Rosinante's feet. After beating both knight and squire very soundly, the carriers were afraid of what might follow, so they prudently made off as fast as their legs would take them.

Quixote and Sancho were now in a very woeful condition. The first to recover his senses was Sancho.

'Ah, master, master!' he called out in a feeble and lamenting tone. 'Sir knight—O, sir knight!'

'What is the matter, brother Sancho?' asked Quixote in the same doleful tone of voice.

'I am sorely hurt,' complained Sancho. 'I wish I could get some cure for my bruises. You tell me a true squire mustn't complain, but truly I can't help it!'

'Ah,' sighed Quixote, 'if only I had some of the balsam of Fierabras! That would cure us soon enough.'

'Balsam of what, your worship?' asked Sancho.

'The balsam of Fierabras,' explained Quixote, 'is a healing lotion which I have read of in one of my books of adventure. All the great knights of old were cured of their wounds by its magical properties. Why, only two drops of it would put you right in a few minutes.'

'It's a pity your honour didn't bring some of it with us,' said Sancho Panza. 'We could have done with a drop or two, if you ask me.'

'I swear to you on the faith of a knight errant that within two days I shall have some of this balsam,' said Quixote.

'Two days!' cried Sancho. 'Why, how long do you think it'll be before we can get up and walk? For you don't suppose anybody's going to bring us this precious ointment of yours while we lie here, do you?'

'I shall get it somehow,' answered the knight. 'But this disaster is all my fault. I should not have attacked such a pack of base country clowns. No doubt the god of knights errant has brought down this beating upon me as a punishment for meddling with men who are no true knights. Now, listen to me: in future, when we come upon such a party of low-born ruffians, warn me that I must not attack them, but let you do all the attacking.

51

For you are no knight and may safely fight with low-born ruffians without breaking the rules of chivalry.'

'Thanks very much, your honour!' said Sancho. 'So I'm to do all the fighting. No, Sir, I must tell you plainly that I'm a man of peace, a man with a wife and children to support. I can't go round knocking gangs of twenty or thirty men about just to obey the laws of chivalry. So far as I'm concerned, I freely pardon all the wrongs that were ever done to me, past, present and to come.'

'Friend Sancho,' said Quixote, 'you are a coward. You will never live to possess an island at this rate. Why, suppose I were to make you the governor of some kingdom, how do you think the people would obey you if you were not a man of valour and strength?'

'Yes,' sighed Sancho, 'I do indeed wish I were a man of valour, but I suppose we must take ourselves as God made us.'

'Don't imagine,' said Quixote, 'that I too am not sorely hurt. What would I not give to have some of the balsam of Fierabras! I too could give myself up to despair and die here where I lie, but my duty as a knight errant and my oath to the peerless Dulcinea may not be denied, and for their sake I must take courage and continue to live, if I may. Why, what reason is there for supposing that fortune will not change, and that the sun will not come out from behind the black cloud that has settled upon us? Now, Sancho, let us look to our steeds, for it seems to me that they too have suffered in this adventure.'

'Rosinante's in a pretty poor condition, sir,' said Sancho, 'but my ass is still all right.'

'Ah, I am glad to hear it,' cried Quixote. 'Now, try to get to your feet and see if you cannot get me upon the back of your ass. Then you shall lead me to the road, that we may go and find some castle where I may be cured of my wounds.'

Poor Sancho, with many groans and curses, struggled to his feet and with great difficulty succeeded in saddling Dapple. Then, very slowly and painfully, he managed to assist his master to his feet and get him on to the ass's back, where he sat, or rather lay, in great pain and misery. Rosinante, meanwhile, had also got to his feet, bruised and battered as he was, and Sancho tied him to the ass's tail. Then the whole procession was led slowly along until they regained the road.

Some distance farther on, they found a wayside inn, which Don Quixote was convinced was a castle.

'Castle or inn, it's all one to me,' sighed Sancho wearily, 'so long as we can get some help there.'

The landlord of the inn, seeing Don Quixote laid across the ass, asked what was the matter. Sancho, not wishing to say they had had a fight with some carriers from Yangues, told him that his master had fallen from a steep path on to some rocks.

'Bring him inside,' said the landlord, 'and we'll do what we can for him.'

The landlord's wife, being a kind and charitable person, told her pretty daughter to help her look after the poor gentleman. There was at the inn a servant girl from Asturias called Maritornes, who was a half-blind dwarf, and she too helped by making up a bed for Quixote in a dark and dirty hay-loft at the top of the inn, where a carrier also slept. The bed consisted only of some rough planks laid across a pair of trestles, and the bedding was thin and poor. There was a hard mattress full of lumps and a pair of coarse sheets, together with a counterpane whose every thread you could easily have counted. Upon this sorry bed they laid Quixote, and the landlord's wife and daughter bathed his wounds and put plasters on them.

'What is the gentleman's name?' Maritornes asked of Sancho Panza.

'He is Don Quixote of la Mancha,' the squire replied, 'and he is a knight errant.'

'Whatever is a knight errant?' asked the girl.

'Goodness me, what ignorance!' said Sancho. 'A knight errant is one who is soundly beaten one day and becomes an emperor the next. One day he is conquered in a fight and the next day he has islands and kingdoms to give away to his squire.'

Presently the landlord's wife and daughter went downstairs, leaving the servant to bathe and dress

Sancho's wounds, which were no less severe than his master's. Then Maritornes bade him good night and went downstairs.

Later, when knight and squire were somewhat rested, Quixote told Sancho to go down and ask the landlord for the things to make up the famous balsam of Fierabras.

'Ask him,' said Quixote, 'for oil, wine, salt and rosemary.'

'Very good, my lord,' said Sancho, and groped his way downstairs.

The innkeeper, who was dozing in the room below, got out what Sancho required and came upstairs with him to see what the knight did. Quixote rose painfully from his bed and mixed the wine and oil together in a basin. Then he added the salt and the rosemary and held the basin over the fire to warm it.

'Now,' he said, 'I shall need a glass bottle in which to keep the precious liquid.'

But no glass bottle was to be found, so the innkeeper fetched him a cracked earthenware jug; and into this, muttering prayers and holy words in Latin, the knight poured the mixture. But the jug would not hold all he had made, so he decided to try it on himself instantly. Holding up the basin in his hands, he poured what was left down his throat. Almost at once he was violently sick, and such a cold sweat broke out all over his body that he asked to be covered up and kept warm. The innkeeper and Sancho helped him back to bed and covered him with all the clothes they could find. Whereupon Quixote soon fell asleep.

In three hours' time, cured of his fever, he awoke, feeling much refreshed and rested.

'Why, friend Sancho,' he said, 'I am healed. This must

be the effect of this wonderful balsam of Fierabras. Heaven be praised!'

'Will my lord allow me to take a little?' asked Sancho, who had had no sleep and was still in great distress. 'For indeed, I have wounds that need curing, just like your lordship.'

'Assuredly,' answered Quixote.

So Sancho took a great draught of the medicine, and instantly felt so ill that he thought his last moments had come. He went pale in the face, trembled all over and began to groan and twist about in his misery.

'Now, this comes of your being no knight,' said Quixote. 'Undoubtedly this precious and magical liquid ought not to be used on such as are not knights. I fear the effect upon an ordinary man is by no means good.'

'Then why on earth,' asked Sancho indignantly, 'did your worship allow me to drink it?'

Quixote did not heed his squire's protest, but instead rose up and put on his armour as best he could.

'Come friend,' he said, 'I am completely recovered and am impatient to be on my way. For the world is full of wrongs to be righted, and how shall people see great deeds of knighthood and combats with giants and dragons if we linger here?'

So saying, he strode downstairs, to be greeted by the landlord, who asked if he had slept well and presented him with the reckoning. He demanded to be paid for food and lodging and for the stabling of horse and ass.

Quixote was surprised to hear such a demand from one whom he supposed to be the governor of a castle.

'Why no, sire,' he said, 'let not such matters be spoken of between such as you and I! I am a great and noble knight, and I cannot be expected to pay in vile money for what is my right. How could wandering knights manage to live if they had to pay for their entertainment wherever they went?'

'I know nothing about that,' said the landlord. 'All I know is, I want my money.'

'Sir Knight,' said Quixote, 'I have been well entertained and cared for at this fortress, and I would reward you in a manner fitting a knight of my quality. If you have any enemy in the world or any who has done you wrong and whom you would have me slay, or bring in chains to your feet, you have only to name him. I, Don Quixote, knight of la Mancha and servant of the gracious lady Dulcinea of Toboso, will be happy to perform this service for you.'

The innkeeper said he didn't need anyone killed, he simply wanted his bill paid. At which Quixote indignantly turned away, mounted his horse stiffly, bade his host farewell and rode out of the inn yard, bidding Sancho follow him.

The host now turned upon Sancho and ordered him to pay the bill his master had refused to pay.

'By no means,' said Sancho. 'I obey the same laws as my master. If he can't pay owing to the rules of chivalry, no more can I!'

He was about to mount his ass when a party of tradesmen who happened to be at the inn and had listened to all that went on, decided to make sport with Sancho, for they thought the landlord had been badly treated.

'Pay up, you rogue!' they said.

Then they seized poor Sancho and fetched out a blanket from the inn. Four of them took hold of the corners of the blanket, and the others threw Sancho upon it, and he was tossed up and down until he shouted for mercy. Hearing the shouts, Quixote turned back and called upon the men to leave his servant alone. But they took no notice, until at last, tired of the sport, they let Sancho out of the blanket and helped him on to his ass. The girl Maritornes, who also took pity on him, brought him some water; but Quixote, who by now had returned to the inn yard, offered him some of the balsam of Fierabras, which he still carried in the jug.

'Here,' he said, 'though this precious liquor is reserved for true knights, I will spare you a few drops of it, to cure you of your hurts.'

'Take your precious medicine to the devil!' cried Sancho. 'It was the cause of half the trouble.'

So Quixote rode away, and Sancho followed him on Dapple. He had forgotten to take his leather saddle-bags, and these were kept by the landlord in payment of the reckoning.

So ended that adventure.

— 6 —

The Adventure of the Flocks of Sheep

Sancho followed dolefully after his master, so shaken and battered that he could hardly sit upon his ass.

'I tell you what, Sancho,' said Don Quixote when his squire had caught him up, 'I am now sure of one thing: that castle was enchanted.'

'You don't say so!' said Sancho. 'I never thought of that.'

'You may depend upon it,' continued his master, 'it was in the power of my unseen enemy, the foul enchanter who strives to thwart me in all my exploits. I am certain that those fellows that tossed you in the blanket were not men, but spirits or hobgoblins. Otherwise I should have come to your aid and given them the punishment they deserved.'

'Well, that's as may be,' said Sancho. 'Hobgoblins or men, it makes little difference, for I was sorely bounced.

If you ask me, they were no spirits but men, like you and me, and if I could get at them I'd enjoy having my revenge, I can tell you.'

'You are wrong,' said Quixote; 'these ruffians were hobgoblins in the service of the enchanter.'

'Well, that's neither here nor there,' said Sancho. 'But if you ask me, these wonderful adventures you go about looking for, they bring us nothing but trouble, and the best thing we can do is to jog along home and look after our own business. Why, so far we've had nothing but blow after blow and bruise after bruise. It's all very well for a knight errant like yourself, who can be cured with magical medicines and is too grand and noble to fight with common folks. But how about me? Why, I get knocked about by hobgoblins as you call them, so that I can't even get my own back on them!'

'Poor Sancho!' cried Don Quixote. 'I fear you have a low and cowardly spirit, and do not understand the glory of knight errantry. How can we be different from ordinary men if we only do as they do? The world is full of adventures to be undertaken and wrongs to be righted—of enchanters to be overcome and foes to be vanquished: how are these things to be achieved if we linger at home in sloth and ease?'

'Well, for my part,' grumbled Sancho, 'I could do with a bit of sloth and ease just now.'

'What I require,' went on Quixote, as if absorbed with his own thoughts, which were always of chivalry and mighty deeds and not of broken bones and bruised bodies—'what I require is a sword of magical power, such a sword as was carried by the great Amadis of Gaul —"the burning sword" he called it. And not only had it power to ward off giants and enchanters, it had an edge

like a razor, to pierce through the toughest armour ever
made. With such a sword I should be proof against all
enchantments!'

'It's all very well for you, sir,' said Sancho, 'but what
about me? If your worship *did* find a sword like this—
and I dare say you will find one growing on the nearest
blackberry bush—it wouldn't do *me* any good! It would
be just like your famous balsam of what-d'you-call-it—no
use to anyone but a true knight.'

'Ah me, Sancho,' said Quixote, 'I fear you have none
of the spirit of adventure in you.'

So they went on, talking and arguing, until suddenly
Quixote raised himself up in his saddle and looked towards the horizon on the right-hand side of the road. A
cloud of white dust was to be seen, moving slowly across
the landscape.

'Why look, Sancho!' cried Quixote, his face lit up by
joy and excitement. 'See you yon cloud of dust? It is
raised by a prodigious army marching this way, and
composed of an infinite number of nations.'

'If that's the case,' answered Sancho, looking towards
the horizon on the left-hand side of the road, 'there's two
armies, your honour, for there's just as great a dust over
there!'

At that, Don Quixote looked and was overcome with
delight, firmly believing that two huge armies were ready
to engage each other in the plain before them, for his
imagination was so full of battles and enchantments that
his mind turned everything he saw into what he wanted
to see. So he was quite unable to see that what he thought
was two mighty armies was nothing but two flocks of
sheep, and that it was nothing but these same peaceful
creatures that had raised the dust.

Now it was not possible to see the sheep at such a great distance, so thick was the dust they had raised upon the road; so Sancho was easily persuaded by his master that the flocks were indeed two mighty armies about to engage in battle.

'What's to be done, sir?' inquired Sancho.

'Why, this is the day of days!' cried Quixote eagerly. 'This is the day upon which my fame shall be raised to the skies and echoed throughout the four quarters of the world! You ask what is to be done? My reply is—assist the weaker side in its fight against the stronger. See you, friend Sancho, yon army upon our right side is led by no other than the great Alifanfaron, Emperor of the vast island of Taprobana. The other that advances on our left is his enemy, the King of the Garamantians, named Pentapolin of the Naked Arm—so called because he always enters into battle with his right arm bare.'

'Fancy that now!' said Sancho Panza. 'But tell me, sir, why are these two great captains going to fight each other?'

'It is like this,' answered Quixote. 'Alifanfaron is a heathen prince, and he desires to marry the beautiful daughter of Pentapolin. But Pentapolin refuses permission unless his adversary agrees to change his religion and become a Christian.'

'Quite right too,' said Sancho. 'Pentapolin is in the right, and I will do my utmost to help him.'

'Well said, Sancho,' said Quixote. 'You are right— and in such a battle any man may fight, be he a knight or no!'

While the two flocks of sheep, still covered in a dense cloud of dust, approached nearer, the knight and his squire rode to the top of a slight hill in order to view them better. Then Quixote proceeded to give Sancho an account of all the great and famous knights who he said were fighting on either side. Their names were supplied from his wonderful memory, which was stuffed with the tales of chivalry and enchantment he had been reading; there was scarcely a province in Spain, a country in Europe, a nation in the whole world which had not sent its bravest princes and leaders to fight in the armies of Pentapolin and Alifanfaron that day. Not only did Quixote tell Sancho their names, he described their armour and the devices on their shields; and not only did he name brave knights, but also magicians and giants as well. In short, Sancho was so carried away by his master's tale that he almost believed it.

'But sir,' he said at length, 'how if all these great kings and chiefs you mention are not kings and chiefs at all, but enchanters and spirits like them hobgoblins who tossed me in the blanket?'

'No, no, friend Sancho!' cried Quixote excitedly. 'Do you not hear the neighing of their steeds, the music of their trumpets and the beating of their drums? Listen!'

Sancho listened. He was in no doubt whatever as to what he heard.

'Master,' he cried, 'what you call the noise of horses and drums and trumpets sounds to me for all the world like the bleating of sheep and lambs.'

And so indeed it was, for the two flocks were by now so close that their bleating was unmistakable. Indeed, Sancho could by now make out some of the sheep and lambs, as well as their shepherds. But Quixote paid no heed, so carried away was he by his tale of princes and giants, and so eager for the battle that was to bring him everlasting glory.

'Sancho,' he cried, 'I see that you are afraid. I cannot blame you, for the approach of two such mighty hosts might well daunt any but the bravest. I am not daunted, but eager for the onslaught. Stay here and watch how I shall cover myself with honour in defence of the great Pentapolin, this true Christian warrior!'

So saying, he couched his lance, set spurs to Rosinante's bony flanks, and charged down the hill-side towards the nearer of the flocks. In vain did Sancho Panza call out:

'Master, O master, come back, I beg you! Yonder are no knights and giants but only sheep and lambs. There's no glory in fighting them, only trouble with the shepherds. Come back, I say! You're mad, sir—do you hear?—mad, I say!'

Don Quixote uttered a ferocious war-cry in a voice of thunder which could be heard over the whole plain:

'Ho, knights and men of the mighty Christian king, Pentapolin of the naked arm, hither am I come, Don Quixote of la Mancha, to succour you in your fight against the dastardly and godless Alifanfaron of Taprobana. Now all of you, be of good heart and fall upon your enemy. Victory shall be ours!'

The shepherds were dumbfounded at the appearance of Don Quixote, who they were convinced was stark mad, and the sheep and lambs put up very small resistance. They could do nothing but bleat the louder, as the ferocious knight charged amongst them, spreading slaughter and bloodshed in his path.

'Follow me, knights of Pentapolin!' cried Quixote. 'See how I avenge the cowardly insults offered by the heathen foe to your master!'

The shepherds called out to him to stop, but he took

no heed, so they began to attack him with stones hurled from their slings. These he heeded not, but called out loud:

'Where art thou, ungodly and hateful Alifanfaron? Show thyself in person and let the renowned Don Quixote, flower of chivalry and pride of la Mancha, challenge thee single-handed to mortal combat!'

Then he went on laying about him with all his might, until a big stone hit him squarely in the side and stove in two of his short ribs.

Quixote at first feared he was slain, but then he remembered the magical balsam of Fierabras which he still carried with him in a broken jug. Taking out the jug, he was about to drink from it when another stone hit his hand, broke the jug, which fell in pieces to the ground, and knocked out three or four of the knight's teeth. This blow was indeed serious, and Quixote toppled from the back of Rosinante and lay in a heap on the earth.

At this the shepherds were afraid, for they feared they had killed the mad stranger; so as quickly as they could they rounded up their flock and made off, leaving the dead and wounded, seven sheep in all, strewn on the plain.

As soon as the shepherds and their sheep were at a safe distance, Sancho rode Dapple down the hillside and went to the help of his master.

He had been watching with despair in his heart, tearing at his beard with anger and vexation. Now he stood over the knight, shaking his head.

'O sir,' he said, 'what did you go and do it for? Couldn't you see they were nothing but sheep? Didn't I warn you? Didn't I tell you to come back? Why couldn't you have listened to me?'

'Ah Sancho,' replied Quixote, 'that shows how cunning is my enemy! For do you not see that these sheep, as you call them, were armed warriors in disguise? Ignorant as you are, I could hardly expect you to know this. But you must learn that the knights and giants who follow Alifanfaron, that wicked king, have power to transform themselves into what they will—even sheep and lambs if they please. I beg you now, Sancho, only follow them a little way upon your ass and you shall see them change back into knights as soon as they think we are not looking.'

Sancho was so angry at his master's refusal to see the plain truth that he felt he could do no more. He went some distance away and leaned miserably upon the back of Dapple, deep in thought.

'There's nothing for it,' he told himself. 'The man's a fool and nobody can do anything for him. He hasn't an ounce of common sense. These adventures of his have caused nothing but trouble. The only thing I can do is to leave him and find my way home as best I can. God keep me out of knight errantry for the rest of my days!'

Quixote, meanwhile, had pulled himself painfully to his feet by means of Rosinante's bridle, for the good nag had never left his master's side, but stood by him silently all the time he lay on the ground. The knight staggered up to Sancho and laid a hand on his shoulder.

'Don't be down-hearted, Sancho,' he said; 'good fortune is surely on the way. Neither good luck nor bad luck ever lasts long, and we have had so much bad luck, you and I, that good luck is sure to follow in no time. Come, get out that saddle-bag of yours and let's have a bite to eat, for this great battle has made me hungry.'

'Then your worship looks like being hungry all day,'

replied Sancho, 'for the saddle-bags have gone. I must have lost them at that accursed inn. But your worship is always telling me of the wonderful herbs and roots that are to be found in the fields for the nourishment of wandering knights and squires. If you ask me, we'd better go and find them!'

'Ah Sancho,' said Quixote, 'such things are good enough for men of peace or for knights in love; but just now I'd rather have a slice of bread and two salt pilchards than all the herbs in Spain. Well, we must make the best of it. Come, my friend, get on your ass once more and follow me; and God, for whom we fight, will surely come to our aid.'

Sancho had nothing to say. He just shrugged his shoulders and helped his master on to the gaunt back of the patient Rosinante. Then he mounted his ass once more and followed where Quixote led.

— 7 —

The Great Adventure of the Fulling-Mills

They rode on all day, gathering what food they could find
by the wayside, but nowhere could they discover anything to drink. The afternoon passed, and gradually night
came on. At last when it was almost dark and the stars
began to appear in the sky, they came to a place where
the grass seemed fresher and longer than anywhere else.
Here they stopped and dismounted.

'I'll bet you anything,' said Sancho Panza, 'that there's
water near here. Let's see if we can find it, for if you ask
me, thirst is ten times worse than hunger.'

They led their patient steeds through the dusk, trying
to find the water that made the grass so fresh; and at last
they heard the sound most welcome of all to weary
travellers—the noise of a great waterfall in the distance.
They stopped and listened awhile, to make sure of the
direction from which the sound was coming. Some

minutes passed. Then another noise greeted their ears—one far less welcome than the sound of falling water; it was a noise to strike fear into the heart of the bravest, and especially Sancho, who was not remarkable for his courage.

The sound they now heard was that of repeated blows reverberating with sickening regularity at some distance away from them, mingled with a dismal rattling of iron chains. Add to this the noise of roaring waters and the moaning of the night wind which had sprung up, together with the rustling of leaves overhead, and you will readily understand why the heart of poor Sancho was smitten with terror. The night had only just fallen and dawn was many hours away. Moreover, they were in a place of desolate loneliness where no one was likely to come and relieve them from the frightful danger in which they stood.

Then it was that the courage of Don Quixote, the intrepid cavalier from la Mancha, rose above all danger and fear. He leaped upon the back of Rosinante and, defying the darkness, the whistling wind and the dire noises that had chilled the blood of his squire, he pronounced in ringing tones:

'Know, Sancho, that I was born in this age of iron to restore the age of gold, that fabulous time of which the sages and poets tell. I am the man for whom fate has reserved the most dangerous and formidable exploits, the most stupendous and glorious adventures, and the most valorous feats of arms ever recorded! I am the man who must revive the order of the Round Table, the Twelve Peers of France, and the Nine Worthies of ancient times! Do but observe, my faithful squire, what a multitude of terrors surround us—a horrid darkness, a doleful solitude, a confused rustling of leaves, a dismal rattling of chains, a howling of the winds, an astonishing noise of caratacts that seem to fall from the very Mountains of the Moon, a terrible sound of redoubled blows which wound our ears like thunder, and nothing which can give any hope of relief or assistance to our failing spirits! Well might the valour of Mars himself, God of War, desert him in the midst of such terrors, but the spirit of your master, the illustrious knight of la Mancha, is ever stronger, ever more undaunted. Observe how I undertake this fearful adventure, Sancho! What a stroke of fortune has befallen you, for you shall be witness to one of the most utterly renowned, one of the most eternally-to-be-honoured deeds that shall ever have been performed in the history of the world. You may stay here, while I ride forward. If in three days I do not return, then you may go back home, first stopping at the village of Toboso, where you shall inform my lady Dulcinea of how her true and royal knight perished in this great attempt to bring her everlasting fame and honour.'

At this poor Sancho, who was already overcome by alarm, began to weep pitifully.

'O master,' he begged, 'don't attempt this rueful adventure. No good will come of it. It's quite dark, sir, and nobody's looking. I can easily go without water if you can, sir; so all we have to do is to get out of this place as quick as we can. Oh, it's a terrible place, sir, not fit for man or beast. Haven't you had enough ruinous adventures for the time being, your worship? And you want to start another in the middle of the night, leaving poor me all alone in the darkness and almost frightened out of my wits! Why, sir, didn't I give up wife and home and children, all to follow you? And are you going to leave

70

your poor Sancho to be devoured by tigers? Think of me, sir, only think of me!'

'Enough!' said Quixote sternly. 'Do you not know that Heaven, which gave me the resolution to undertake this adventure, will give me strength to succeed in it? Heaven will protect both you and me, Sancho, you may depend upon it.'

'We haven't done so well up to now, sir,' said Sancho. 'Oh, why didn't I stay at home and not go gadding off in search of islands? I don't want an island, sir, honestly I don't. What would I do with it? Please turn round and let's be off home.'

'I refuse to listen to such cowardly talk,' replied Quixote. 'Come, Sancho, fasten my horse's girths tighter, for I long to begin my great adventure.'

Sancho saw that it was no use to argue, so he decided by some trick to keep his master there until daylight, so that at least he would himself not be left there alone in the dark. Pretending to tighten Rosinante's straps, he tied the horse's hind legs together by means of his ass's halter.

'That's it, sir,' he said, shaking his head ruefully. 'Good-bye, master! I wish you wouldn't do this, but if you must, you must—say a last farewell to your poor squire and be off, sir!'

'Courage, Sancho!' cried Quixote. 'I shall say no farewell, for I feel certain that before many hours are past you shall once more behold me, covered with glory. Forward now, Rosinante!'

But, try as he would, Rosinante could not move. Each time his master spurred him, he could only jump forward a short way, and could by no means charge, as his master commanded.

'There, sir,' cried Sancho triumphantly. 'You see that Heaven is on my side and won't let your horse carry you to your death. I don't suppose any of your famous knights of old tried to go on riding when their horses wouldn't move. Now sir, have some sense, and just wait till morning. Daylight can't be far off, then you can charge along to your heart's content.'

Quixote, fretting and angry, only spurred Rosinante the harder, but the poor beast was quite unable to move.

'Very well,' said Quixote, 'there is nothing for it but to wait till morning—though I am ready to die from impatience. Ah, Sancho, if you had not such a base and cowardly spirit, you would understand how hard it is for a proud knight such as I to be kept from the fulfilment of his heart's desire.'

'It's all right, sir,' Sancho said encouragingly, 'the time will soon pass. I tell you what—suppose I tell you some of my stories—that is, unless you feel like getting off your horse and having a nap on this soft grass.'

'For shame!' cried Quixote. 'When danger threatens, my place is in the saddle. Talk not to me of napping on the grass.'

'Sorry, sir,' said Sancho, 'I meant no harm. I dare say even old Amadis de Whatnot had a nap sometimes. But just as you say, sir.'

'I will remain mounted,' said Quixote, 'while you stand by my side. Now, let me hear some of these stories of yours, that the time may pass more swiftly.'

So Sancho stayed close to Rosinante's side, for fear of the dreadful noises that still fell upon his terrified ears; and one by one he told his master all the tales he could remember. They were not very good ones, most of them, for he never could recollect how they ended. But somehow they whiled away the night, and when the first streaks of dawn were seen in the eastern sky, he yawned with relief and told his master he could talk no more. Without letting Quixote see, he stooped down and untied Rosinante's hind legs, and the horse, delighted to be released, pawed the ground and joyfully sniffed the morning air. Quixote took this to be a good omen, and was eager to begin his great undertaking.

'Once more farewell,' said Quixote. 'Follow after me a short distance, and then await my return. But if I do not return, have no fear about your reward, for before leaving home I made a will, and you shall see that in it you are provided for.'

At this Sancho once more began weeping, for he could scarcely bear to hear of these signs of his master's affection.

'Be of good courage, Sancho,' said Quixote, 'all is not

lost! I may return in triumph, and then you shall certainly have the island I promised you.'

With that he went slowly forward towards the place where the noise of rushing water and heavy blows could still be heard, while Sancho followed after, leading Dapple by the halter.

Presently they came to a green meadow. Beyond it they could see a mass of high rocks, down which fell a great cascade of water. This was the sound that had first attracted their ears to that place. At the foot of the rocks were several ramshackle buildings, which were more like tall barns than houses. Quixote then realized that it was from the inside of these neglected buildings that the hammering sound proceeded. Blow after blow he heard, louder and louder the nearer he approached. What could be going on inside, that could produce such a terrible beating and rattling of chains? As they drew nearer, step by step, even Rosinante hesitated in fear, but his master's soothing tones encouraged him. Quixote all the while called alternately upon Heaven and his lady Dulcinea to come to his aid; and as for Sancho, he clung close to his master, peering through Rosinante's legs in order to see what it was he so much dreaded. No doubt the buildings they were approaching were the abode of some terrible giants or monsters, whom Quixote would attack single-handed, bringing himself to utter destruction, and leaving his defenceless squire to run for his life. The next few minutes seemed like hours, and Sancho's terror and apprehension caused a cold sweat to break out all over him.

Then all at once they came round the corner of a rock and saw what it was that had brought such a great terror upon them. It was neither giants, nor devils, nor monsters.

It was nothing but half a dozen cloth-mills, and the noise of beating and the rattling of chains was made by the great hammers which were raised up by water-power and allowed to drop on to the lengths of cloth beneath. This process is called, in the cloth-making trade, *fulling*—and it is by such hammering and pounding that the cloth is cleaned and thickened. It was these harmless machines that had caused all the night's alarm!

Quixote was dumbfounded, and sat upon his horse unable to move or to speak. He hung his head in shame and disappointment. So this was the end of that great adventure which was to raise his fame throughout the four corners of the world!

Sancho, overwhelmed with relief and seeing his master thus dejected, was ready to burst into a roar of laughter. Don Quixote caught sight of him and could not forbear to break into something like a smile. Whereupon Sancho could contain himself no longer and gave vent to a great peal of laughter, and could scarcely prevent himself from rolling upon the ground. Four times he broke into wild and uncontrollable mirth, and between the fits he cried out:

'So you were born in the age of iron, were you, to restore the age of gold? And you're the man destined by fate to revive the Round Table, the Twelve Peers of France and the Nine Worthies of ancient times, are you? Good job the Nine Worthies can't see you now, isn't it, sir? They wouldn't half have a laugh, they would!'

So infuriated was Quixote by his squire's insolence that he struck him a couple of blows on the shoulders with his lance.

Whereupon Sancho, seeing that his laughter had displeased the knight, begged his pardon.

'Have mercy upon me, your honour,' he said. 'I was only joking.'

'Then I don't like your jokes,' said Quixote severely. 'How was I, a true-born knight, to know the sound of a fulling-mill? No doubt such sounds are well known to low-born fellows such as you, but my life, I am glad to say, has been passed far away from such mean implements of drudgery.'

'Still, you must admit, sir, that this adventure had its funny side. I should think people might well have a laugh out of it, if they knew the truth.'

'By all means,' agreed Quixote, 'and for that reason it would be well for us to keep quiet about this night's affair, for ordinary people do not understand the ways of knight errantry. You had no business to make fun of me, Sancho, but I repent that I struck you. In future I must beg you to show more respect, and I for my part will endeavour to control my passions.'

So knight and squire were agreed, and Sancho promised that in future he would observe the rules by which a squire followed his master, always remembering to treat him with due honour and respect.

The Famous Adventure of Mambrino's Helmet

Just then it began to rain, and Sancho suggested retiring into one of the fulling-mills and waiting till the shower had passed. But Quixote would by no means agree, for he now had a horror of the place where he had been made such a fool of. Accordingly, they struck off from the path and presently reached the highroad. They had travelled scarcely any distance before a sight met their eyes which filled Don Quixote's heart with joy.

'Aha!' cried he. 'Yonder, if I am not mistaken, is a knight riding upon a dappled grey horse with something on his head which I am certain is Mambrino's helmet. Doubtless, friend Sancho, you remember the vow I made concerning Mambrino's helmet.'

This famous object was nothing less than a helmet of pure gold, cunningly fashioned and richly decorated, which Quixote had read about in one of his tales of adventure. It had been worn by a famous pagan named Mambrino; and Quixote had sworn before his squire to obtain possession of it and wear it as his own.

'Take care, master,' said Sancho. 'Don't rush into more mad adventures. We don't want any more fulling-mills, do we?'

'Wretch!' said Quixote angrily. 'A golden helmet is not a fulling-mill! Surely this is one of those cases where fortune, having dealt us one sad blow, makes up for the past by bringing us next morning an adventure which will be crowned with success. Look yonder. Do you not see a knight riding upon a horse of dapple grey with a shining helmet upon his head?'

'What I see,' said Sancho, 'looks uncommonly like a fellow on a donkey—and I wouldn't swear to any gold helmet till I see it closer.'

'I tell you, that's Mambrino's helmet!' exclaimed Quixote excitedly. 'Stand at a distance, Sancho, and let me deal with this knight. Watch me, I say, and see how I waste no words, but possess myself of this priceless treasure.'

'I'll stand at a distance all right,' said Sancho, 'but as for the helmet, let's hope it doesn't turn out just another fulling-mill.'

'Don't mention those mills again, or I'll pound you into a jelly, do you hear?'

Now the truth of the matter was this. There were in those parts two villages, one of which was so small that it had not even a shop. There was no barber to attend to the needs of the villagers, so that one from the larger village was in the habit of travelling between the two. He happened just now to be on his way between his own village and the smaller one, and he was wearing a new hat. When the rain came on, he placed his barber's basin on his head to keep his hat dry. It was newly polished, and to Quixote's imagination the barber and his grey ass just as easily took on the shape of a wandering knight upon a dappled steed.

Don Quixote, at the approach of the unfortunate barber, immediately couched his lance and charged straight at him, crying out with all the strength of his lungs:

'Base slave and coward wretch! Yield unto me that which is mine by right!'

As soon as the barber heard these terrible words and saw the ferocious knight thundering down upon him, he very prudently did the only thing which would save his life: he fell off his ass. When Quixote's charge had spent itself, he scrambled to his feet and ran off across the fields as fast as his legs would carry him, leaving his ass and his basin behind.

'So,' cried Quixote, 'I am master of the field! Sancho, take up the helmet!'

'Not at all a bad basin,' said Sancho, 'and well worth having, if you ask me.'

He handed it to Quixote, who put it on his head, turning it round and round to find the visor.

'What an enormous head the wearer of this must have had,' said Quixote.

Sancho smiled to think that his master should take a barber's brass basin for a golden helmet.

'What are you grinning at now?' asked Quixote.

'I was smiling to think what a big head the heathen must have had,' said Sancho. 'You know, sir, if you ask me, this helmet, as you call it, looks uncommonly like a barber's basin.'

'To you no doubt it would,' said Quixote. 'But to me who can see things as they are, it is undoubtedly the enchanted helmet I have been looking for. I believe that someone must have had it cut in two and sold half of it for gold, so that the remaining half does indeed look something like a basin. But that is no matter. As soon as we come to a town where there is an armourer, I shall have it altered to fit me. Meanwhile, I shall wear it as it is, and no doubt it will at least protect me from sticks and stones.'

'Well, perhaps it may,' said Sancho, 'unless they're thrown from slings, like the stones at the battle of the sheep that knocked your honour's teeth out, and broke the jug with the famous balsam of what-d'you-call-it in.'

'As for the balsam of Fierabras,' said Quixote, 'the

loss of that is of no importance whatever, for I carry the recipe for it in my head.'

'So do I,' said Sancho, 'and shall do as long as I live! If ever I make that stuff, or drink another drop of it, may I be struck dead and give up the ghost. Pretty near poisoned me, it did!'

'Sancho,' said Quixote, 'if you were a true Christian, you would endeavour to forget the ills that have befallen you and think upon the future.'

'Very well,' agreed Sancho. 'Now sir what about the future of that poor fool's donkey, which he has run off and left to look after itself. Do you think we might stick to it? For, by my beard, it's not a bad animal.'

'It is not my custom,' said Don Quixote, 'to plunder those whom I overcome; nor is it usual among us knights for the victor to take the horse of his vanquished enemy and let him go afoot, unless his own steed be killed or disabled in the combat: therefore, Sancho, leave the horse, or the ass—whatever you please to call it; the owner will be sure to come for it as soon as he sees us gone.'

'I've a good mind to take him along with us,' said Sancho, 'or at any rate to swop his saddle and bridle for mine, which aren't in too good a state. Why, hang it, sir, surely the laws of chivalry can't prevent a chap from swopping his saddle and bridle for another man's, when the other man's run away.'

'I am not absolutely sure on that point, Sancho,' said Quixote, 'and therefore, until I am better informed, I give you permission to make the exchange, provided you can assure me it is absolutely necessary.'

Having his master's leave, Sancho exchanged the grey ass's trappings for his own, which were nothing like so good. Then master and squire made their breakfast from such scraps of food as they had left, and drank at the stream which drove the fulling-mills. But Quixote would not look back towards the mills, for the shame of his encounter with them was still strong in him. Accordingly, they remounted their beasts and rode on along the high road, allowing Rosinante to determine their direction, as is the custom with true knights errant. As for the grey ass, he followed patiently along behind Sancho Panza.

— 9 —
How Don Quixote freed the Galley-Slaves

As Don Quixote and Sancho Panza journeyed on, they
saw approaching them in the distance a party of about
twelve men fastened by their necks to a long chain, and
with handcuffs on their wrists. They were marching in
sorrowful procession guarded by four men—two on
horseback armed with muskets, and two on foot armed
with swords and pikes.

'Now who can they be?' asked Quixote, who had never
seen their like before.

'They look like men bound for the galleys,' said
Sancho, 'where they'll be forced to row in the King's
service.'

'Forced?' asked Quixote. 'Does the King *force* men to
work for him?'

'It's not so much the King as has forced them,' said
Sancho, 'it's their own crimes and misdoings.'

'I do not like to see men forced,' answered Quixote. 'I believe there is work for me here. No true knight may see injustice done without desiring to put it right.'

'I don't know so much about injustice,' said Sancho. 'These men are criminals, your worship. You don't want to have anything to do with them.'

By now the knight and his squire had come up with the foremost of the slaves. A sorry crew they looked, dragging the long chain that fastened their necks together, their lean bodies showing through their rags.

'I will speak to the chief of the guard,' said Quixote, riding up to one of the two men on horseback. 'Permit me, kind sir, to ask of you what is the nature of these men's offences, that they are chained and bound in this way?'

The chief of the guard said to Quixote:

'Ask them yourself, señor. They are shameless and hardened criminals, and I do not doubt that they will give a true account of themselves.'

Don Quixote then addressed himself to the first of the gang of slaves, a thin, shifty individual who eyed him slyly.

'What have you done, friend, that you should be led away in chains to toil in the King's galleys?'

'My crime, sir,' said the man, 'was being in love.'

'Being in love?' repeated Quixote. 'Surely that is no crime. I myself may say that I am in love with the peerless Dulcinea, the most beauteous lady in all Toboso.'

'It was no lady I was in love with,' said the man. 'It was a basket of linen. I loved it so much that I stole it, and wouldn't be parted from it till the officers came to take me. For which crime, sir, I am committed to the galleys for three years.'

'I see,' said Quixote gravely; and then, turning to the

next of the unfortunate fellows on the chain:

'And what about you?' he asked. 'Are you, too, guilty of being in love with other people's linen?'

'No, sir,' said the second man, a most dejected creature whom all the other men seemed to despise. 'I am sent to the galleys for singing.'

'For singing?' repeated Quixote. 'But that is no crime! Upon my honour, if a man can be punished only for singing, there is great injustice in the world.'

The guard explained.

'Singing, señor,' he said, 'means, in the language of these rogues, confessing under torture. This is something for which all men despise a criminal, however guilty he may be. This man confessed under torture that he had been a cattle-stealer, and for this he has been given two hundred lashes and six years in the galleys.'

The third man confessed that he had been sent to the galleys for five years for stealing ten ducats.

'Ten ducats?' said Quixote. 'Why, I will give you twenty if that will free you.'

'Alas!' replied the prisoner. 'It's too late. My sentence is passed, and I must suffer it.'

The next two slaves were an old man, a pitiful creature who had been convicted of practising black magic; and a student who had been found guilty of forging money.

Quixote's attention was then caught by the sight of a squint-eyed young man of about thirty, who was more tightly chained than all the others. Their wrists were fastened with handcuffs, but this man's hands were pad-locked to his sides so that he could not move them in any direction. Quixote asked why.

'He has committed more wrongs than anyone else,' explained the guard. 'He has been sentenced to ten years in the galleys, and he is none other than the famous Gines of Pasamonte.'

At this the man began to insult the guard in loud and boisterous language, so that the guard was about to strike him for his insolence. But Quixote intervened and prevented him from bringing down his staff on the prisoner's back.

'Permit me,' he said, 'to beseech you not to strike this defenceless fellow. Since his hands are tied, it is right that his tongue should be free. Listen to me, gentlemen,' continued the knight, addressing all four guards. 'I am a member of the noble order of knighthood, and I cannot permit these men to be maltreated by those to whom they have done no wrong. They are not your enemies, and I must beg you to release them instantly. If you do not comply peaceably with my demands, I shall be constrained to enforce them with sword and lance!'

The leader of the guard laughed aloud.

'Why, this is pleasant fooling!' he said. 'But we can't stand here talking all day. So if you'll be good enough to get out of the way, we'll be on our road.'

'O sir!' began Sancho, who was afraid his master was once more going to start a fight. But Quixote cut him short.

'I warn you,' he said to the guard, 'you had better do as I command, or it will be the worse for you!'

'Out of the way, old fool!' answered the guard contemptuously. 'Put that basin straight on your noddle and stand aside.'

This was too much for Don Quixote.

'You are a cat, a rat and a rogue!' he shouted, and attacked him immediately with sword and lance. The guard was taken unawares, and received a wound in the arm from Quixote's lance. This so pained and surprised him that he fell off his horse and rolled on the ground; instantly, all was confusion. The galley-slaves, seeing their chance to escape, broke their chains and attacked the guards. Sancho Panza released the prisoner Gines of Pasamonte, who ran to the fallen leader of the guard and helped himself to his musket. This he fired into the air

in the direction of the guards, who were at the same time being attacked by a volley of stones from such of the slaves as had managed to free themselves of their hand-cuffs.

Thus taken by surprise, the guards made off as fast as they could, vowing vengeance upon Don Quixote in the name of the King, whose prisoners had been unlawfully set free.

By now Sancho was thoroughly alarmed. He knew

that the guards would call out the nearest officers of the peace, and a search would be made for his master and himself. If they were caught, they could expect little mercy from the King's officers, who would certainly not listen to Quixote's nonsense about knight errantry and the duty of freeing slaves. Accordingly he begged his master to leave the place and take refuge in the woods until the search had been given up.

'I will consider what is best to be done,' said Quixote, 'but first I must address the men I have freed.'

So he called the jubilant galley-slaves about him and spoke thus:

'Gentlemen, it is natural for a man of good birth to feel gratitude, and no crime is more hateful than ingratitude. I well understand how deeply obliged you must feel towards me for what I have done, but the only reward I desire from you gentlemen is this—that you take the chain from which I have just freed you to the town of Toboso and there, presenting yourselves before the peerless lady Dulcinea of Toboso, tell her that her faithful servant, Don Quixote of la Mancha, has commanded you to wait upon her and to assure her of his unspeakable reverence and devotion. Then you shall give her an exact account of this famous achievement, by which you once more enjoy the sweets of liberty. When you have done this, I give you leave to seek your fortunes where you please.'

The men were astonished at this request, and a murmuring broke out among them. Gines of Pasamonte answered for them all:

'Sir,' said he, 'what you ask is impossible. To go together in a band to Toboso would be certain death. The King's officers will be on our track immediately, and our only hope of escape is to separate and go singly into the woods and hills until the pursuit dies down. I can assure you, we haven't the slightest intention of putting ourselves in chains again, and that's what would happen if we took the high road together. I'll tell you what, though,' he continued, 'instead of going and paying our respects to your lady Dulcinea, we'll all promise to go into the next church we find and say a prayer for your honour's success.'

At this Quixote was furious.

'Base and ungrateful wretch!' he cried. 'You, Gines de Pasamonte, shall take the whole chain by yourself and lay it at my lady's feet, as a punishment for your insolence.'

By now Gines was convinced that Quixote was out of his wits, so he called upon his fellow prisoners to attack him. They were in no mood to argue, so they prepared to assail the knight and his squire with stones. Quixote set spurs to Rosinante, but the poor beast was so frightened that he refused to move. Sancho in fear and trembling hid behind Dapple. Quixote and Rosinante were quickly felled to the ground. Then the prisoner who had been a forger of money tore the knight's helmet from his head and began to beat him over the shoulders with it. Then he threw it to the ground and jumped on it till it was battered out of all recognition. Next he stole the doublet with which the knight covered his armour, and another stripped poor Sancho of his cloak. Then all the prisoners whom Quixote had freed made off as fast as they could in all directions—all directions, that is, except that of Toboso, which was one place in Spain they vowed would never see them.

Sancho was the first to recover himself. He brushed the dust off his remaining clothes and tightened the straps on his donkey.

'Master,' he said, 'I beg you, do as I said. There's no time to lose. The officers will be after us in no time. Come, give me your hand.'

He helped Quixote to his feet, while Rosinante also struggled up from the ground. Then Sancho picked up the barber's basin which had been so badly treated, and did his best to restore it to something like its original shape.

'Ah, Sancho,' said Don Quixote sorrowfully, 'this is what comes of helping base-born wretches! I should have had nothing to do with them. They are monsters of ingratitude. Having rescued them, I should certainly have taken your advice and left them alone. But now I have learned my lesson. How could I suppose that such miserable rogues and villains would understand the ancient customs of knight errantry? Is there anything in the world worse than ingratitude, Sancho?'

'I'm sure I don't know, sir,' said Sancho. 'If you will

91

go meddling with thieves and murderers, you must expect to get yourself into trouble. But now, if you're ready, sir, let's be pushing on. The further we get from this place, the happier I shall be.'

So Quixote, murmuring sadly about the ingratitude of men, climbed stiffly into the patient Rosinante's saddle and turned the horse's head towards the distant mountains. Sancho gladly followed his master.

— 10 —
The Dispute at the Inn

For some time Don Quixote and Sancho Panza wandered
at large in the woods and mountains, until at length they
reached the self-same inn where Sancho had been tossed
in a blanket. Once more they greeted the landlord, his
wife and daughter, and the servant Maritornes. Then
Don Quixote settled down to enjoy food and rest, while
Sancho began to clean and repair the ass's trappings
which he had taken from the barber.

It so happened that at that very moment the barber
himself came into the inn yard. He at once recognized
Sancho as the servant of the knight who had robbed him
of his basin.

'Oho!' he cried. 'So I've caught up with you at last,
have I? And if I'm not mistaken, you accursed thief and
highway robber, isn't that my ass's saddle you have?'

So saying, he laid hands on the trappings and was

about to attack Sancho, when the squire, angered by the barber's language, grasped the saddle with one hand and hit the barber a blow in the face with the other.

The barber kept hold of the saddle and cried out so loudly that the whole inn was alarmed at the noise and scuffle.

'Help, help!' he shouted. 'I demand help in the King's name, for this rogue has robbed me on the high road, and now he's trying to murder me for taking what belongs to me!'

'That's a lie!' cried Sancho. 'I didn't steal his saddle. My master Don Quixote won it from him in fair fight.'

By this time Don Quixote himself had appeared, and was listening to his squire with approval. He now considered Sancho to be a man of spirit and resolved to knight him at the first opportunity.

'Upon my honour,' he said to himself, 'such a man as this would do credit to the noble order of knighthood!'

'Gentlemen,' called out the barber, addressing himself to those who had come out at the noise of the quarrel, 'I am ready to swear this is my ass's saddle. I know it as well as I know my own face! Moreover, this very day these rogues robbed me of it, they also took away a new basin which I had only just bought for the sum of five crowns.'

At this Quixote could restrain his anger no longer. He stepped between the squire and the barber and, seizing the saddle, laid it on the ground for everyone to see; then he addressed the onlookers as follows:

'This saddle, gentlemen, is beneath my notice, but you may judge of the claims of this fellow, this ignorant barber, by what he says of the famous Mambrino's helmet, which I took from him in battle. This sacred helmet is made of pure gold and is of great antiquity, and he calls it a barber's basin! After the fight, my squire begged leave to take this coward's saddle and trappings for his own steed, and I gave him permission. In confirmation of my words, Sancho, run inside instantly and fetch the helmet of the great Mambrino!'

Sancho tried to persuade his master not to produce the helmet, which he swore everyone would recognize as a basin.

'Silence!' ordered Quixote. 'Run and do as I command.'

As soon as Sancho had brought the basin, Quixote held it aloft for all to see.

'Gentlemen,' he cried, 'here is the helmet I spoke of, and which this ignorant rascal demeans by calling a basin! It is the self-same piece of armour which I won in combat, and it has been in my keeping ever since.'

'That I can swear to,' put in Sancho, 'for my master has worn it ever since the battle, and since then he only fought in it once: that was when he freed the galley-slaves, and the ungrateful wretches would have taken his life, had not this same honest basin-helmet protected his brains from the stones they threw at him.'

Now it was the barber's turn to speak.

'Come, gentlemen,' he said, addressing the onlookers, 'let us hear your opinion. I call upon you for confirmation—is not this a basin which the gentleman calls a helmet?'

At this a man stepped forward who happened also to be a barber. This second barber decided to make the most of the fun, so he looked at the basin gravely and said:

'I am sorry to have to disappoint you, my honest friend. I have been a barber myself for thirty years, so that I know all the tools of our trade. I have also been a

soldier in my youth, and I think I know a helmet when I
see one. Now it is my honest opinion that this which you
call a basin is certainly a helmet—though,' he added, 'I
am bound to admit that it is not a *whole* helmet.'

'You are right,' said Quixote, 'for the visor is missing.'

'A clear case!' cried a priest who was among the
onlookers, and the others echoed him. 'Of course it's a
helmet—anyone can see that!'

At this the poor barber was quite distracted.

'Well, if so many honest men,' said he, 'are convinced
that my basin is a helmet, I suppose it must be. But I'm
amazed that there should be another man in all Spain
except this madman here who doesn't know a barber's
basin when he sees one! And if my basin is a helmet,
then I suppose my ass's saddle must be a horse's trappings
too.'

'As to that,' said the priest, 'I think we should have
the opinion of Don Quixote, for no other but a knight
errant is fitted to decide in such a matter.'

At this everyone laughed, and Quixote answered:

'Nay, gentlemen, such strange things have happened
to me since I arrived at this castle that I am persuaded
everything here is enchanted. I think it best that the
question should be decided by the assembled company,
whose understandings may not have been subject to so
much disturbance as mine. Of the nature of the helmet I
am perfectly convinced, but as to whether the saddle is
an ass's trappings or a horse's, I cannot truly say.'

'He is right!' cried a gentleman called Don Fernando.
'Let us put the matter to the vote. I will ask everyone's
opinion privately and see how you decide.'

Some of the company, who knew of Don Quixote and
his adventures, found the jest very amusing, but others

considered it great nonsense. Among these were three of the King's officers who had come into the inn in search of various wrong-doers. Don Fernando went the round of everyone in the yard, asking their opinion; and at last he pronounced judgment:

'Honest but misguided fellow,' he said, addressing the poor barber, who was by now at his wits' end, 'everyone in the assembled company has now given it as his opinion that the object before us, which you call an ass's saddle, is in reality the saddle of a horse, and a very richly appointed horse into the bargain. I must accordingly award it to the person from whom you endeavoured to take it not so long ago.'

'For my part,' said the barber, 'I am neither mad nor drunk, and I believe you are all mistaken. Nevertheless, I have lost my basin and my saddle by due process of law, so I must bid them farewell.'

Many were amused at this, but one man, a servant, spoke up for the barber.

'Come,' he said, 'the jest has gone far enough. Anyone can see that the helmet is a basin and the saddle is the saddle of an ass. Let the fellow have what belongs to him!'

It was now the turn of the King's officers to interfere.

'He is quite right,' said one of them. 'I don't know what sort of foolishness is going on here, but anyone who is not mad or drunk can see that this is nothing but an ass's pack saddle. Let it be restored to its rightful owner.'

'You lie, you unmannerly knave!' cried Quixote, and aimed a blow at the officer with his lance. The officer stepped aside, and the lance was shivered to fragments against a wall. Then the officer called upon everyone to assist him in the King's name.

Instantly everything was in turmoil. The officers tried to lay hold on Quixote, and Don Fernando and his men came to the knight's rescue. The barber took advantage of the confusion to seize his saddle, but Sancho, who had been watching him, fell upon him, and once more the two were fighting for all they were worth. The priest cried out, the officers continued to call upon the whole company for assistance, the landlord ran inside for his sword, and his wife, his daughter and the servant Maritornes screamed 'Murder!' The whole inn was a medley of curses, screams, kicks, blows, bloodshed, disorder and alarm.

At the height of the pandemonium Quixote became convinced that he was in the middle of a great attack upon an armed camp which he had read about in one of his books. So he cried out in a voice of thunder which caused everyone to stop and listen.

'Ho, everyone!' he shouted. 'Lay down your arms and cease to destroy each other! Let peace be restored, for there is no use in this senseless slaughter!'

But the King's officers, who had been knocked about a good deal, were by no means satisfied. One of them suddenly recalled that he had in his possession a warrant for the arrest of the scoundrel who had freed the galley-slaves and so perverted the King's justice. He took out the warrant and read out the description of Quixote contained in it.

'Gentlemen!' he cried. 'I call upon you to assist me in the execution of my duty. Sir, I arrest you in the King's name!'

Whereupon he grasped the knight by the collar. Quixote, thoroughly angered by this action, seized the officer by the throat and would have strangled him but for the intervention of the men in the crowd.

'Base rogue!' cried Quixote. 'You should not talk of arresting knights errant! What I did in releasing the galley-slaves was but common justice. Knights errant cannot be tried by common law or accused of perverting justice, for they are themselves the instruments of justice! Go home, sir, and leave me in peace!'

The priest persuaded the officer that Quixote was mad, and that no magistrate would convict him, whereupon the officer was obliged to leave Quixote alone. The dispute between Sancho and the barber was settled by the barber's retaining possession of the saddle and Sancho of the girths; and as for the basin, the priest himself paid the barber for the loss of it.

Peace being thus restored and differences composed, the whole assembly went their several ways and calm once more fell upon the inn where so many alarms and adventures had befallen.

— 11 —
More Adventures at the Inn

While they were staying at the inn, Don Quixote's mind was very much taken up with a story he had heard about a certain Princess Micomicona, who had been shut up in a castle far away by a fierce and terrible giant. He was convinced that it was his duty to slay the giant and rescue the Princess, although he had never set eyes on her.

Now it happened that Quixote was lodged in a room in which the landlord had hung a number of wine-skins— that is to say, the leathern vessels in which in those days it was customary to keep wine. They hung about Quixote's bed, for the room was cool and dark, so that it made a good store-house for wine.

One night Quixote's mind had been so running on the Princess Micomicona that he went to sleep in a fevered and confused state. He dreamed that the giant had come into his very room. The knight immediately seized his sword, although he was still fast asleep, and began attacking the wine-skins, which he mistook for the giant.

'Ho, there, sir giant!' he cried. 'Now is your last hour come! On guard, you miscreant traitor, or this very moment shall be your last! Defend yourself, and prepare to do battle with the renowned cavalier of la Mancha, sworn protector of the weak and powerless!'

With these and other wild threats he called out in his sleep, and so disturbed Sancho that he ran into the room with a light to see what was wrong with his master.

'Take that, you hideous monster!' cried Quixote. 'Huge as you are, I shall have the better of you!'

With that he plunged his sword into the largest of the wine-skins, which was at once cut down from the hook where it hung and rolled on the floor, spurting red wine in all directions. Not content with this, he attacked the other skins, shouting out wildly and calling upon all true Christians to help him in his battle against the giants—for by now the one giant had grown into several, and Don Quixote, in his disordered dream, was bent on slaying them all.

Sancho rushed from the room and aroused the landlord and his wife. Maritornes and the landlord's daughter were already awake. They all listened breathlessly to Sancho's tale. With eyes starting out of his head, the squire, who like his master was convinced that the inn was enchanted, told how his master was engaged in killing giants, and had called on everyone for help.

'He has drawn his sword,' said Sancho, 'and is tackling them all single-handed. Never did you see such a rumpus in all your lives! The floor is swimming in blood. He has done for two or three of them already.'

'The man is mad!' said the landlord. 'You're both

101

mad, master and man—stark, staring mad!'

'Not a bit of it,' said Sancho. 'Come quickly, or my master may be killed. Why, I saw one of the giant's heads with my own eyes. Rolling about on the floor it was—bigger than the biggest wine-skin in Spain.'

'Wine-skin!' cried the hostess. 'Why, that's what he's up to, is he, the old lunatic? Depend upon it, husband, he's destroying our wine-skins.'

Everyone rushed out of the room and up the stairs. In the doorway of the knight's room they stopped, for there they saw the most ridiculous thing imaginable. Quixote, still half asleep, and with an old greasy night-cap of the landlord's upon his head, was kneeling on the bed, laying about him with his sword, while the damaged wine-skins hung above him or lay on the floor, amidst pools of wine.

'Oh, my poor wine-skins!' said the hostess. 'What harm did the poor things ever do you?'

'Take that, you rogue!' cried Quixote. 'Ah, you thought you could escape me, did you? Here's for you, you blackguard! What makes you think you are a match for the great Don Quixote, who lives only to defend the unfortunate Princess!'

The landlord in fury attacked Quixote with his fists, but the knight took not the slightest heed. He went on slashing at the skins with his sword, so that the landlord had the utmost difficulty to avoid losing an ear or a hand himself. They might have continued like this all night, had someone not brought Quixote to his senses by throwing a bucket of cold water over him. Immediately he awoke from his nightmare and dropped his sword. Then he sank back on the bed, saying feebly:

'Where am I—Oh, where am I?'

'You're in my house,' answered the landlord, 'which was a decent respectable place till you set foot in it! Look what you've done to my wine, you villain!'

Sancho meanwhile had been searching the room for the giant's head, which he was sure he had seen rolling about in a sea of blood. At last he realized what had happened, and looked at the mess all round him with dismay.

'Dear, oh dear!' he said sadly. 'Here's a nice business. Away goes my island—I don't suppose I shall ever get it now!'

While the hostess, her daughter and the servant did their best to clear up the mess, the landlord continued to work off his fury.

'Never you mind about islands,' he said to Sancho. 'What about my wine and wine-skins? Who's going to pay for this lot, I ask you? A curse upon the laws of knight-hood, which allow madmen to wander about the country-side breaking up other people's houses and not paying a penny for all they eat and drink! I don't care a rap for the laws of knighthood—this crazy old savage shall pay for every penny-worth of damage he's done!'

Don Quixote seemed to understand little of this. Although he was now awake, he was by no means in his right mind and was still convinced that he had slain at least one giant, if not several. Suddenly he sat up and stared around him. Then, perceiving Maritornes, whom he did not seem to recognize, he fell at her feet and said:

'O matchless Princess Micomicona, receive the sub-mission of your protector, who has done battle against those fearful giants who assail you! Behold the blood of your enemies, with which my sword is stained. Never in the history of knighthood has there been such a great and

memorable encounter. Deign to look with favour upon the prostrate form of your sworn defender!'

He continued to utter more nonsense of this kind, while Maritornes and the landlord's daughter gently helped him to bed once more. Whereupon he instantly fell back upon the pillow and was soon fast asleep. The company then went off to renew their interrupted slumbers, the landlord and his wife vowing vengeance against the man who had caused them so much trouble.

Next evening Don Quixote, fearing that some of the supposed giants had escaped and might return to get possession of the Princess, decided to stay on guard all night. It was useles for Sancho to try to persuade him to stay in bed like a sensible man.

'Friend Sancho,' said Quixote, 'you may sleep, for you are a common man and have no need to watch, as I have.

But it is my duty, as a member of the order of knight-hood, to stand all night outside this castle and ward off intruders. Good night. My place is on my gallant horse!'

So saying, he took sword and lance and mounted the patient Rosinante. Then he rode out of the inn yard and the gates were locked behind him. Don Quixote sat motionless upon Rosinante until all was quiet in the inn, and the moon rose in the sky.

'O lady Dulcinea,' said Quixote out loud, 'wherever thou art, give an ear to the prayers of the sorrowful knight who has thee ever in his thoughts. Perhaps even now thou art looking at this same moon and musing upon thy absent adorer.'

In the meantime Maritornes and the landlord's daughter had made up their minds to stay awake and listen to Quixote's speeches, for they had heard he was to mount guard all night, and they knew his habit of mutter-ing to himself. They had never in their lives heard such flowery language. So they went to an upper room whose window overlooked the place where Quixote stood in the moonlight, moaning quietly to his absent Dulcinea, and sitting upright on the back of Rosinante, his lance resting on the ground and supported by his right hand.

After the two girls had listened for a while, they determined to play a trick on the knight. Maritornes ran downstairs and obtained possession of the halter belong-ing to Dapple. When she got back to the room where the other girl was waiting, she called out softly from the window:

'Come a little nearer, sir knight, that my mistress may see you and overhear your fair speeches.'

Don Quixote turned Rosinante towards the window and stood beneath, looking up at the landlord's daughter.

She thanked him graciously and begged him to speak to her. Now Quixote imagined that she was the daughter of the governor of the castle, and that she was madly in love with him.

'Alas, fair lady,' he said, 'my heart is already the prisoner of my far-off saint, the lady Dulcinea of Toboso. She is my queen, my star, the flower of all my life and the object of my hopes. To her must I be for ever faithful, as becomes a true and worthy knight.'

'Sir,' answered Maritornes, 'only allow my mistress to touch your hands, for if she can get no relief she may run mad, and her father, should he hear of her love for you, may cut off her ears or do some other terrible act!'

At this Don Quixote could hardly refuse, so he stood upon the back of Rosinante, immediately below the window, and raised his two hands for the maiden to touch. Instantly Maritornes slipped one end of the halter over his wrists, pulled it tight, and fastened the other end to the lock of the door. Then, scarcely able to keep themselves from laughing out loud, they left the room and went back to bed. Quixote found himself unable to move. He immediately became certain that he had been enchanted, for he could not imagine anyone's deliberately playing a trick on him. If he moved, Rosinante might take alarm and run away, leaving him hanging by his wrists from the window.

'Let me go, I beseech you!' he cried in piteous tones.

But there was no answer, and he was forced to stand upon Rosinante's back until the moon sank behind the clouds and the first signs of dawn appeared in the east. He called upon his lady Dulcinea to come to his aid, and then he besought the help of all the magicians he could think of. Next he called out to Sancho, but his squire was snoring soundly, well out of earshot. So the knight cursed his fate, and bewailed the day that ever he had come to the enchanted castle. As morning broke, Quixote was sure that both he and Rosinante were bewitched, and he began to fear that his punishment would be eternal.

'So this,' he said, 'is the end of all my adventures and the failure of all my hopes. May the lady Dulcinea in her infinite kindness pray for the soul of him who died in her service.'

Just then a party of four horsemen, who were riding early, arrived at the inn and demanded admittance.

'Honest cavaliers,' exclaimed Quixote, 'it is useless for you to seek admittance to this castle until it is day and the governor awake! Then he will know if your are fit persons to come within his walls.'

'Nonsense!' said the leader of the horsemen. 'This is an inn, and a pretty poor one too. Are you the landlord?'

'Do I look like a landlord?' asked Quixote.

But the question was in vain, for in the half-light he could not be seen distinctly.

'We're in a hurry,' said the horseman. 'We need refreshment for ourselves and our horses. Let us in at once.'

So saying, he went up to the gate of the inn and began beating on it. His companions dismounted, and one of their horses trotted up to Rosinante to greet him. The horse sniffed at Rosinante, and Rosinante sniffed at the horse; and together they trotted a little way from the inn to smell the morning air. Rosinante forgot about his master, so that poor Quixote was left hanging from the window by his wrists. He began to bawl out for someone to come and rescue him from his pitiable situation.

Quixote's cries and the battering of the horseman at the gate soon aroused everyone in the inn. The landlord ran down to let the travellers in, while Maritornes, guessing what had happened, slipped quickly into the room where she and the landlord's daughter had looked out of the window, and unfastened the halter that bound Quixote's wrists. The knight dropped to the ground outside the window just when the landlord and the horsemen had come up to see what all the shouting was about.

'Whatever's the matter now?' asked the landlord.

'I have been most unjustly enchanted in this accursed castle!' said Quixote. 'I demand satisfaction. I will challenge to the death anyone who denies what I say.'

The four horsemen were amazed, and the landlord explained to them as best he could what sort of man Quixote was.

But the knight would listen to him no longer, and

strode into the inn yard, calling loudly for his squire. Sancho was already in the stable attending to Dapple.

'Come, Sancho,' said Quixote. 'We must not stay a minute longer in this evil and inhospitable fortress. Let us be off!'

So without further speech with the landlord, and without more delay, they left the inn for the second time. And those at the inn were not sorry to see them go.

— 12 —

The Adventures of the Goatherd and the Penitents

Meanwhile Don Quixote's friends in la Mancha were still worried about the knight's exploits, for they feared he would come to some serious harm. Bitterly they cursed the books of knight errantry which had been the cause of all the trouble. At length the priest and the barber were persuaded by Quixote's niece and his housekeeper to go in search of him and bring him home, by force if necessary. So they hired a wagoner to fill an ox-cart with straw and go with them to find Quixote. Sancho's wife, too, was out of temper at her husband's long absence.

Not long after the knight and his faithful squire had left the inn, they were greeted by the priest and the barber, who persuaded Quixote, much to Sancho's joy, to go home with them.

'But first,' said the barber, 'let us rest and refresh ourselves. We've brought food and wine. Let's sit down in this pleasant spot, in the shade of the trees, and have our meal.'

So the four of them sat down in the shade, and the barber spread out a cloth he had brought with him, and on the cloth he laid cold meat, pasties, bottles and glasses, cakes and fruit. Just as they had begun to eat and drink, they heard the sound of a little bell; and turning round, they saw that a black-and-white she-goat had appeared out of a thicket, pursued by her goatherd, who was trying to capture her.

'Come, my pretty one,' the goatherd was saying, 'why have you strayed from home like this? Come back with me and wander no more. Oh, how like a girl you are, who never can learn sense, but will be always doing as she wishes and taking no heed of her friends' advice.'

'How right you are, fellow,' said the priest, for all were much amused by the goatherd's words. 'Since this creature is a female, she will do as she likes; so why be in such a hurry to force her back to the fold? Come, friend, sit down and eat with us, and tell us something of yourself.'

'I thank you,' said the goatherd, who was a well-spoken young man of good appearance. He took his seat upon the grass and accepted the leg of a rabbit which the barber handed him. 'You may think me silly for talking to a goat like this, but I'm not such a fool as I look. If you will listen, I'll tell you my story.'

'By all means,' said Quixote. 'There may be an adventure here, and I can assure you that these gentlemen, like myself, will listen with interest.'

'If you don't mind,' said Sancho, 'I'll take this pasty away and eat it by myself over yonder. I've heard enough stories for the time being, and it's far more important for

111

a squire to eat while he can. I may not get a chance like this for a week.'

So saying, he removed himself and the pasty some distance away, while the goatherd began his tale.

His name, it seemed, was Eugenio. He and Anselmo, another young man from his village, had been rivals for the love of a certain rich farmer's daughter, named Leandra. The girl was beautiful and amiable, but alas! her heart was turned by the appearance in their village of a handsome young man of the name of Vincent de la Rosa. He claimed to have returned from the wars in distant lands, and his uniform was bedecked with medals and trinkets of little value but impressive appearance. All the villagers listened to the tales of his imaginary heroism, which soon came to the ears of the beauteous Leandra. Not only was the gentleman a great talker, but his figure was gay and dashing in the extreme. He had indeed only three suits, but by wearing part of one with part of another, and varying the colours of his stockings and his plumes, he contrived to give the impression of having an immense and costly wardrobe. He was in reality a poor adventurer in search of a fortune, and he had lost little time in finding out about the riches owned by Leandra's father. She had been unable to make up her mind between Eugenio, our goatherd, and his rival Anselmo; but now she quickly forgot both, and, to make a long story short, she consented to run off with Vincent de la Rosa, having first got possession of her jewellery and money, which were in the care of her father. As soon as he discovered his daughter's flight, the poor father was distracted and sent out a party of armed men to recover her. Vincent had led her away into the mountians, taken her jewels and her fortune and abandoned her in a lonely cave. As soon as

112

she was brought home, her father instantly had her shut up in a nunnery, where her friends and admirers could neither see nor talk with her.

'So you see, gentlemen,' said the goatherd, 'why I appear to be out of my mind, and why I call to this goat, which behaves so like my sweetheart Leandra, to come back to me and let the past be forgotten.'

Here he heaved a deep sigh, and everyone sighed in sympathy.

Then Don Quixote, who had listened to the goatherd's tale with an expression of the utmost sorrow, spoke:

'Brother goatherd,' he said solemnly, 'I am a knight errant and it is my duty to assist the afflicted. I have heard your story with the most profound concern, and I can assure you that if it were in my power to do so, I would instantly gird on my sword, mount my peerless steed, and attack the nunnery wherein your lady is so cruelly imprisoned. Then, notwithstanding all that the abbess and her followers might do to prevent me, I would release the lady Leandra and deliver her into your hands, to do what you liked with, only reminding you that it is against the laws of chivalry to offer violence to a woman. How fortunate you are to have encountered the one man in all Spain best fitted by destiny and merit to perform great deeds of knighthood in succouring the weak and resisting villainy! Be assured, sir goatherd, that in due time I shall be at hand to undertake the relief of your wrongs.'

The goatherd was amazed at Quixote's words, as also at the knight's appearance, for up to now he had scarcely noticed him. Don Quixote's gaunt and sorrowful face, his bent and rusty armour and his generally ramshackle air struck him as ludicrous in the extreme.

'Who's this old scarecrow?' he whispered to the barber, who was sitting next to him.

'Why, don't you know?' said the barber out loud. 'This is no other than the great and famous warrior, Don Quixote of la Mancha, the righter of wrongs, the foe of giants and wizards, the champion of distressed maidens.'

'H'm,' said Eugenio, 'sounds like a lot of story-book nonsense to me. I take it, sir,' he went on, speaking to Quixote for the first time, 'that either you're making fun of me or you've got a screw loose.'

'You are a rogue!' answered Quixote angrily. 'That is no way to speak to a member of the knightly order. I have more sense in my head than ever you will have! Take that!'

Whereupon he seized a loaf of bread that lay on the cloth and threw it full in the goatherd's face and hit him on the nose. Eugenio had no intention of taking this lying down. He sprang to his feet, leaped over the table-cloth and grasped the knight by the throat. He would undoubtedly have strangled him but for Sancho Panza, who had come to the aid of his master, and now pulled the goatherd backwards on to the table-cloth. Dishes and glasses were smashed by his fall, and the food was scattered about in all directions. Quixote, freed from the goatherd's grasp, had jumped upon him and began pummelling him with all his might. The goatherd, who was younger and nimbler than his adversary, readily got the upper hand once more. Tearing himself free, he immediately sat on Don Quixote and began belabouring him in turn. The rest of the company were roaring with laughter, having never before seen such a diverting scrap. How it might have ended no one could tell, for suddenly a sound was heard in the distance—a sound so melancholy and mysterious that everyone stopped to listen. It was the noise of a trumpet, blown dolefully on the other side of the valley.

'A truce, a truce!' panted Don Quixote. 'Only grant me relief for one hour while I see what is the cause of yonder solemn music. Here, if I mistake not, is business for me.'

Eugenio had had enough of fighting and willingly let Quixote rise. The knight then perceived approaching down the path a party of men in white bearing before them the figure of a woman dressed in deep mourning.

Now the truth was this. For a whole year there had been no rain, and all the people of the countryside were anxious for their crops and their cattle. If rain did not come soon, they would lose everything they had and many would die of thirst. Accordingly, prayers were offered up everywhere, and pilgrimages made to holy places to ask the saints to assist them in their desire for rain. The procession in robes of white which now appeared was on its way to a hermitage not far off, and the figure they carried before them was the image of the Virgin Mary draped in black. To Quixote, however, the men in white were false knights, and they were carrying off some unfortunate lady to imprison her in an enchanted fortress, where she would perish of misery and starvation in a dungeon.

So he strode resolutely to where Rosinante was thoughtfully munching the grass, and climbed into the saddle. Then he took down his shield from the branch of a tree and called to Sancho for his sword.

'Now,' he cried, 'let all men see how fortunate it is that the illustrious Don Quixote of la Mancha lives to right this wrong, whether or no he perish gloriously in a desperate exploit reserved by fate for his accomplishment. Down with the miscreants who have seized you, helpless damsel! Come to my aid, O peerless Dulcinea, flower of Toboso, for never has your sworn knight undertaken so perilous a task!'

With that, he seized his sword from Sancho, braced his shield before him, and dug his heels into Rosinante's bony sides, for by now he had lost his spurs. Then he urged the patient nag to a comfortable jog-trot in the direction of the procession; for never in this whole history can it be recorded that Rosinante advanced at a gallop.

The squire, the priest and the barber were overcome with dismay at the knight's actions and urged him to desist.

'Sir,' cried Sancho, 'O dear master, come back! These

are no knights but only a procession of priests and villagers, and the figure they carry is no damsel in distress but an image of Our Lady, the property of the Holy Church. Leave it alone, sir, I implore you!'

But in vain. Quixote was bent on pursuing the adventure and took no heed whatever of his squire's entreaties. He rode up to the leaders of the procession and brought Rosinante to a standstill. Indeed the horse was already feeling like a rest, so that Quixote had no difficulty in checking him.

'Listen to me, sir!' said Quixote sternly to the procession.

'If you have anything to say,' answered one of the priests who had been engaged in singing a chant, 'say it quickly, for we must be on our way.'

'I was born to redress evils,' announced Quixote, 'and I order you, on pain of my extreme displeasure, to release that unfortunate lady, whose tearful face and melancholy garments prove that she has been carried away against her will.'

At this the men took Don Quixote to be some foolish wanderer who had lost his wits, and they laughed outright. This so angered the knight that he drew his sword and attacked one of the men carrying the image. The man, a sturdy village labourer, instantly drew one of the poles which were being used for carrying the image and attacked Quixote with it, giving him a blow across the shoulders which made him tumble from Rosinante's back and roll on the ground.

Sancho Panza called out to the man to leave Quixote alone, as he was only a poor gentleman who did not always know what he was doing; and the man did so, not because of what Sancho said, but because, seeing Quixote lying

117

still on the ground, he was afraid he had killed him. Whereupon he ran away across the valley and was soon out of sight.

By this time the priest and the barber had also come up, and those at the head of the penitents recognized the priest from la Mancha, who was able to explain to them why Don Quixote had attacked them. They then showed concern for the poor knight's condition, and on looking down at him they saw Sancho kneeling beside him making a most piteous lamentation.

'O flower of chivalry,' he wailed in the way he imagined his master would have spoken at such a moment, 'O pattern of knighthood and brightest ornament in all la Mancha! Now thou art gone, who is left in the world to redress wrongs and succour the feeble? Oh, why hast thou left thy faithful squire alone in this hard world, to mourn the kindest master that ever drew breath? Why ever did you go and do it, sir?'

The sound of these words revived the knight, who raised himself painfully on one elbow.

'Peerless Dulcinea, rose of all the world,' he murmured, 'where am I? Ah Sancho, I think it is time we were going home. Help me, I beg you, on to yonder wagon, for I fear I am in no fit state to bestride Rosinante.'

Sancho, overjoyed to see his master alive, although in a piteous condition from the blow he had received across the shoulders, said:

'That will I do gladly, your honour. Then we'll be off home at once, where you can prepare for further adventures that may turn out better than this last one.'

'You are right, Sancho,' agreed Quixote. 'At present the stars are unfavourable. We will wait at home until a more favourable star is in control, so that our next undertaking shall turn out more favourably.'

So Sancho, the priest and the barber helped Quixote on to the wagon and made him as comfortable as possible on a bed of straw. Then, bidding farewell to the members of the procession, and with Sancho leading Rosinante by the reins, they made off slowly in the direction of la Mancha.

On the sixth day they reached home, and as it was a Sunday all the people were standing in the square in the centre of the village. They were amazed to find that the man lying upon the straw in the ox-wagon was none other than their neighbour Don Quixote. A boy ran off to tell the housekeeper about her master's return. When he told how pale and thin Don Quixote was as he lay upon the straw, the housekeeper and the niece raised a pitiable lamentation, and once more called down curses upon all books of chivalry. Their expression was even more doleful when the wagon drew up at the door of the house, and they saw the poor knight for themselves.

The two women lost no time in getting him to bed, and he lay there looking woefully at them, not quite sure of who they were or where he was. The priest drew the niece aside and told her to watch her uncle very carefully to see that he did not sally out again, since he and the barber had been at such pains to bring him home. The niece thanked him for his advice and said she would do as he bade.

Sancho's wife, Teresa, meanwhile, hearing that her husband had returned and was at the house of Don Quixote, followed him there. As soon as she saw him she said:

'Here you are, husband. How is the donkey?'

'Very well,' answered Sancho. 'A good deal better than I am.'

'Well, that's something,' said Teresa. 'I've missed you both. Have you brought me back a petticoat, or shoes for the children?'

'I have not,' said Sancho. 'A man doesn't ride out on knightly adventures in order to bring back petticoats and children's shoes. But I have something better for you, and you shall see it when we get home. One of these days, my dear,' he continued as they walked back towards their cottage, 'I shall be the governor of an island, and you shall be queen. Then all your subjects will call you "My lady". How will you like that, eh?'

'Fancy that now!' said Sancho's wife, who had only the vaguest idea what he was talking about. 'And how soon will that be, I should like to know?'

'Why, the very next sally which me and master make,' said Sancho, 'he has promised me an island. You shall see. Ah, it's a great life to be the squire to a knight errant and go on adventures. True, nine times out of ten you get knocked about or tossed in a blanket, but believe me, my dear, there's nothing like it in the world!'

Chatting together in this way, Sancho and Teresa jogged along with Dapple following behind.

— 13 —

Don Quixote and Sancho at Home

For some weeks the priest and the barber did not go near
Don Quixote for fear of reawakening in him those
thoughts of knight errantry which had proved so disastrous before. Instead they besought his housekeeper and
his niece to watch him carefully, to keep him quiet, to
feed him well so that he might regain his strength, and to
do their best not to let any books of knighthood and
adventure fall into his hands.

You may perhaps wonder why they took so much
trouble to keep him from harm when he seemed determined to run into all the danger he could find. But they
had a great respect and affection for Quixote, and did not
consider him altogether right in his mind. They blamed
his books for having made him restless and foolish, and
they believed that if only he could forget these books,
and the extravagant stories with which they were filled, he

would recover his senses and return to the quiet life of a country gentleman.

When they paid him their first visit to see how his cure was progressing, they found him dressed, not in his battered armour, but in a green baize apron with a red cap on his head; he looked well, but very lean and shrivelled. They asked after his health, and were glad to note that he talked cheerfully and sensibly.

Then they spoke of ordinary matters, such as the weather and the harvest, until the priest ventured to make some remark about the news of the day.

'Have you heard,' he asked, 'that the King is expecting a great invasion by the Turks, and that everywhere there are preparations for war?'

Now this was a harmless enough remark, but Quixote's answer showed that he had by no means got rid of the notions of knight errantry with which his head had been stuffed.

'Is that so?' he said. 'Then let me tell you, there is one thing that the King of Spain ought to do—and if I could speak to him, I would tell him so in person.'

'And what is that?' asked the barber.

'Why,' said Quixote promptly, something of the old fire coming into his faded eye and a touch of colour to his withered cheek, 'he should issue a proclamation summoning together all the knights errant in Spain! Who can think but that there would be a great concourse of brave and chivalrous heroes who would gladly take up arms against the heathen, as they did in the days of Amadis of Gaul? It is well known that only *one* knight may fight against a hundred thousand and put them to flight by the strength of his arm and the valour of his spirit. Why, I myself——'

123

Here Don Quixote's niece gave a cry of despair. 'Alas!' she cried. 'I might have known it. He is not cured of his foolish notions and is determined to go off again on one of his adventures. Why, uncle, I thought you had given up being a knight errant.'

Don Quixote turned to his niece with a look of mild surprise in his eye. Then he said with dignity:

'Niece, I shall live and die a knight errant.'

'Then there is no hope for any of us,' said his niece.

'How do you suppose,' asked Quixote, 'that having once taken the oath of knighthood, I can ever forswear it? I must go wherever my duty calls me.'

At this moment there was a loud knocking, and the niece and the housekeeper went to the door to see who had come, while the priest and the barber remained to reason with the knight.

The caller was Sancho Panza. He had come to inquire after the health of his master and to find out whether he was thinking of going in search of further adventures.

'Ah, rogue!' cried the housekeeper as soon as she saw him. 'How dare you show your face in this house after the terrible misfortunes you have brought upon my master?'

'What's this?' asked Sancho. 'How can you blame me for what has befallen the gentleman? Is he not in good health?'

'Until he went rambling with you,' said the house-keeper, 'he was as sensible and quiet a man as any in la Mancha. It must be you who has taken him away from home and led him astray in this manner.'

'What rubbish!' said Sancho hotly. 'I went with him because he asked me. It was not I who led him astray. It was he who persuaded me to leave my house and my wife

124

and children to follow him on his mad rambles. And you dare to blame me?'

'Well, you can't come in here,' said the housekeeper. 'Go home and stay as far away from the master as you can get.'

'No, let him in,' ordered Quixote, who had heard the end of this conversation. 'It is kind of him to call and inquire after my health, and it is only right he should be allowed to see me. A squire may at all times have access to the knight he serves.'

So Sancho was admitted, and the niece and the housekeeper were sunk in despair, for they thought it was now only a matter of time before master and squire would once more go off on their perilous adventures.

'They'll never come back!' wailed the niece.

'Or if they do,' sobbed the housekeeper, 'they'll be so battered and bruised that we shan't know them!'

Presently Quixote and Sancho were left alone together, the priest and the barber having taken their leave, for they realized that it was no good their staying while Quixote was in his present excited state.

'Sancho,' said Quixote gently but firmly, 'you should not have blamed me for leading you astray, as you call it. Many men in your position would consider it an honour to be chosen as the squire to so illustrious a knight as myself.'

'It was the fault of your housekeeper, sir,' answered Sancho. 'She made me lose my temper. For my part, I'm happy to serve your honour, especially as your honour has promised me an island for my pains.'

'Tell me,' continued Quixote, 'what do they say of me in the village?'

'Well, sir,' answered Sancho, 'you mustn't be angry

125

with me if I tell you the truth. Most of them think your honour is stark mad. There's some who think you were born dotty, and some who say it's come over you through reading books. Some are sorry for you—others just laugh.'

'I see,' answered Quixote. 'Of course you can hardly expect such people to understand the ways of knight errantry. However, in spite of all they may say, Sancho, I am thinking of starting my adventures again, now that I am recovered. There are still wrongs to be righted and glorious deeds to be done.'

'Quite right, sir,' agreed Sancho heartily. 'If your honour is not displeased with me, I'll be willing to go with you to the ends of the earth.'

But Sancho's wife Teresa was by no means so pleased when she understood what Sancho intended to do.

'My dear,' announced Sancho in the high-flown style used by his master, 'it is possible that I may resume the path of adventure and once more take up my destiny as servant to our illustrious wandering cavalier.'

'Talk plain,' said Teresa. 'Since you took up knight errantry, I haven't understood a word you've said.'

'Quite right,' said Sancho, 'for the words of knight errants are not meant to be understood by common people. To speak plainly, wife, I've a mind to go rambling again with my master, so see that my ass is well fed and cared for, and there's plenty of food to put in the saddlebags. I'm not going hungry this time.'

'It's all very well for you to go gallivanting off all over the country, but you might think of me. What have I got to live on while you're away?'

'The payment I expect for my services is the island I've been promised. Have you forgotten I said I'd make you

a governor's lady and a person of great consequence?'

'That's all very fine. What do I feed the children on in the meantime? Now look here, husband, you tell that master of yours to give you a regular decent wage. He can't expect to get a servant for nothing.'

Sancho thought there was sense in this, so he decided to speak to Don Quixote about it.

Meanwhile the niece and the housekeeper began again to beseech Quixote not to go rambling any more. But he would not listen to them, so they determined to go and speak to a young scholar who lived in the neighbourhood, called Samson Carrasco.

'He is a learned man from the college at Salamanca,' said the housekeeper, 'and surely master will listen to him.'

So she put on her veil and went to talk to Samson

Carrasco. The young man listened patiently and then said he would go and have a talk with Don Quixote. But he did not promise to make the knight leave off wandering.

When Sancho asked Quixote about the matter of his wages, Quixote looked at him thoughtfully for a few moments and then said:

'Friend Sancho, I would willingly give you a weekly wage for your services if I could discover that any of the famous knights of old had done such a thing. I have read almost all the books of chivalry, and nowhere does it say that a squire receives money for his services.'

'I dare say not,' answered Sancho, 'but what is my wife to live on while I'm away?'

'The upkeep of your miserable cottage can cost but little,' replied Quixote. 'She can work, as other women do, and God will look after her.'

'By the hairs of my beard!' exclaimed Sancho. 'Aren't you satisfied with what I've done for you? It seems to me that if I haven't displeased you, I'm entitled to a bit of cash for the time I spend looking after you.'

'A true squire,' said Quixote, 'must only think of the honour and glory he achieves by sharing the adventures of his master. I shall in the end, like other knights errant, reward my loyal servant with the gift of an island. If, however, you are not contented with this, you have only to leave me. I shall have no difficulty in getting another squire. The world is full of men eager for such an opportunity. I have no desire to force a faint-hearted servant to stay with me.'

Sancho, with tears in his eyes, was just going to protest when the conversation was interrupted by the coming of the young scholar, Samson Carrasco. The housekeeper let him in, and she and the niece followed to hear how he would persuade Quixote to give up his foolishness.

Now Samson had had a long talk with the priest and the barber, and they parted in perfect agreement. The ladies were therefore amazed to hear the words in which the young man now addressed the knight.

'O flower of knighthood,' he said, speaking in the language of chivalry, 'illustrious and thrice-famed knight, I am honoured to have the occasion of some discourse with one whose deeds have been talked of all over Spain. May I have the unforgettable joy of wishing your honour good fortune and prosperity!'

This speech pleased Don Quixote, who was delighted to find a young man who knew the language of chivalry.

'Sir,' said Quixote, 'I thank you for your courtesy. Perhaps you can advise me. These good ladies here, as well as the priest and the barber of this village, have been endeavouring to dissuade me from following my knightly calling, and urging me to abandon the wandering life altogether. What do you think I ought to do?'

The young scholar paused, as if thinking out his answer to this weighty question. The niece went down on her knees to him, and the housekeeper implored him to remember what she had told him.

'O sir,' begged the ladies, 'please try to stop him. He doesn't know the misery he causes us by going off on such dangerous jaunts. Tell him to stay at home, sir.'

But Samson Carrasco ignored them.

'Your excellency,' he said at length, 'in spite of all that these good ladies say, it is my advice that you take up once more the calling of knight errant. Yours is the life of service and of glory. I have been thrilled with the tales of your exploits, and I burn to hear more. Indeed,

if you lack a squire on your next expedition, I myself will
be happy to accompany you.'

'There you are, Sancho,' said Quixote triumphantly.
'Didn't I tell you I should easily find another squire?'

Sancho was by now weeping outright.

'O master,' he said, 'take me. Don't leave your faith-
fullest friend behind! How could I stay at home while
you go wandering off, killing dragons and getting stones
thrown at you and sticks broken across your back? Don't
leave me behind, sir!'

Quixote thanked Samson for his generous offer but
said that the young man should stay at home and look
after his parents. He would gladly take Sancho back into
his service, so long as he did not trouble his master with
useless and unworthy demands for money. Sancho was
overjoyed, and Quixote told him to be ready in three
days. It was in vain for the women to implore Quixote
not to go; it was in vain for them to curse Samson as a
traitor and a snake in the grass. It was settled.
Quixote said he had stayed at home long enough in
idleness, and was impatient to set out once more in search
of glory.

There was only one thing—he needed a new helmet.
Samson Carrasco, highly delighted with the way things
had gone, offered to procure a new helmet himself. He
had a friend who possessed one, although its original
brightness had been somewhat dimmed by rust and
disuse. Still, it could be polished up, and his friend would
be only too pleased to present it to the knight.

Three days later Sancho bade farewell to Teresa and
joined his master on the road leading out of the village.
They set off at dusk, to escape the notice of the women,
and only Samson Carrasco saw them go. He went with

them for a mile or two to wish them success in their new undertaking.

Rosinante, though rested and refreshed by his weeks of idleness, was as gaunt and care-worn as his rider. Sancho's donkey, contented and well fed, bore her burdens without complaint, and in the saddle-bags that jogged at her sides there were provisions in plenty. For while Quixote might feast upon dreams and legends, Sancho was used to more solid fare.

— 14 —
How Don Quixote went to visit the Lady Dulcinea

No sooner had they left Samson Carrasco than Rosinante began to neigh and Dapple to bray. Quixote took this to be a good omen for their future success; and as the ass brayed louder than the horse neighed, Sancho believed that his fortune would be greater than his master's. As they rode on, Quixote said to Sancho:

'I am determined, before seeking further adventures, to pay my respects to the peerless Dulcinea, patroness of all my undertakings and sunshine of my life. Before long we shall reach the town of Toboso, for we are riding in that direction. When we get there, my friend, I shall require you to lead me to her palace. You have been there before, but I have not.'

At this Sancho looked somewhat unhappy, but he said nothing. Now the reason for his unhappiness was this. Some time ago, after the knight and the squire had freed the galley-slaves, they had wandered for a while in the mountains; and Don Quixote had sent his squire with a letter to Dulcinea of Toboso. Sancho had been very unwilling to show himself in the town for fear of the King's officers, so he had destroyed the letter and returned without ever seeing Toboso, much less the princess who was supposed to live there. On his return he had told Quixote of his delivering the letter by night at the princess's palace, and of his receiving an answer by word of mouth. The answer he had made up himself; it was mostly nonsense, at which by then Sancho was becoming very skilled. This had satisfied Don Quixote.

It was unfortunate, however, that Sancho was supposed to know his way to the palace in Toboso, for he had not the least idea where it was. Indeed, he strongly suspected—as was indeed the case—that there was no such thing within a hundred miles of the little country town. For the moment he held his peace.

They spent that night searching the streets, but they could find no sign of the lady's dwelling. Nor was there anyone about in the streets to ask. A tall, dark and gloomy building showed itself at the end of a lane, and Sancho suggested that it might be the palace. But it was the church, and Sancho had no wish to linger about the graveyard in the dark; so on they went towards the outskirts of the town.

Presently they heard a clattering on the cobble stones, and a labourer came along driving two mules before him. They asked him if he could direct them to the palace of the lady Dulcinea, but he shook his head.

'There aren't any palaces round here, sir,' he told Quixote, and went on towards the fields, for dawn was approaching and he was about to begin the day's work.

'I tell you what, master,' said Sancho. 'We don't want to be seen wandering about the streets all day. Let's go out into the country and find a comfortable place to have some food. Then I'll come back by myself and make further inquiries. When I've found the princess, I'll give her your love and tell her you'd like to call on her. Then I'll bring you back her instructions. Don't you think that would be more according to the rules of chivalry?'

'An excellent idea, Sancho,' answered Quixote who, though still eager to behold his lady, was becoming weary. 'Let us do as you say.'

So they rode out of town and presently found a grove of trees in which the birds were beginning to sing their morning hymns. Here they dismounted and refreshed themselves with wine and food. After a while Don Quixote told Sancho it was time he returned to the town to begin the search once more, for he was determined not to leave that place until he had received the blessing of the lady Dulcinea.

Sancho bade farewell to his master and trotted off on his ass. As soon as he was out of sight of Quixote, he dismounted and sat down by the wayside. He began to talk to himself in this manner:

'Friend Sancho,' said he, 'where are you off to? Why, to look for nothing at all—a princess who probably doesn't exist, living in a palace that no one has ever seen. And who are you doing this for? For the famous Don Quixote, knight of la Mancha, rescuer of giants, and slayer of damsels, giver of drink to the hungry and food to the thirsty. And where does this princess live? In a palace in Toboso. Have you ever seen her, my friend? No—nor has my master, for all I can tell. And what will the people of Toboso say, when they find you looking for their princesses on behalf of strange knight errants? They'll probably not like it at all and beat you black and blue. Why, this whole affair is a most villainous piece of nonsense, and more harm than good will come of it.'

So ended Sancho's discussion with himself. He therefore made the following resolve:

'Now, the fact is, my master, though a very brave man and an enterprising knight, is stark mad. Everyone thinks so, and I begin to think so myself. As for me, Sancho Panza, I'm crazier than he is for following him. What does the proverb say? "Birds of a feather flock together." And through wandering about with a madman, I've gone mad myself. That's the truth of it. But I'm hanged if I'm so dotty as to roam about the streets of the town any longer looking for something that isn't there! Why, I'm likely to get myself arrested and locked up. No, I've got a better idea than that.

'My illustrious master is a man who mistakes flocks of sheep for armies and windmills for giants. Why may he not mistake any girl I can get hold of for the peerless Dulcinea, flower of Toboso, etcetera, etcetera? That's the idea! I'll make the first country wench I meet come along with me, and I'll tell him it's the princess. If he says she's no more than a country wench, I'll tell him that one of the magicians he's always imagining has transformed her. If he doesn't believe me, he won't send me off on any more of these foolish errands. If he does—and it's ten to one he will—then the business is ended happily, and we can get on with our knight errantry.'

Sancho was highly delighted with himself for having thought of this ingenious plan. He lingered for some time longer in his place of hiding, so that Quixote would think he had spent the time in searching the streets of Toboso;

then towards evening he was fortunate in seeing three girls on donkeys approaching from the direction of the town. They were country girls dressed in common clothes, and their donkeys were not in great condition; but Sancho thought they would answer his purpose well.

Accordingly he remounted Dapple and rode back to Quixote as fast as he could. His master was sitting astride Rosinante, leaning on his lance, and sighing dolefully. When he saw Sancho, he left off calling upon the name of his absent lady and said:

'Ah, there you are, Sancho. You've been a long time. How did you fare?'

'Sir,' replied Sancho in a state of high excitement, 'this is the day of days, the most red-letter day in the whole calendar! Now are your honour's labours crowned with success! And for this you may thank your faithful squire, the illustrious and never-to-be-forgotten Sancho——'

'Yes, yes,' interrupted Quixote, 'but tell me—have you seen my lady?'

'Indeed I have,' said Sancho, 'yonder she comes with two of her serving-women, mounted upon three gambling hags, and——'

'Gambling hags?' said Quixote. 'No, no—it is "ambling nags" you mean. Princesses and their waiting-women are usually seen taking the evening air upon their ambling nags.'

'Well, gambling hags or ambling nags, it is all one,' answered Sancho. 'What I mean to say is "milk-white steeds". You never saw such horses in your life. As for the princess and her maidens—my word, sir! what a sight they are! Their hair—tresses, I should say—hang down their back like sunbeams; their dresses—I mean robes— defy description, and they are bedecked with gems and jewels like what your honour never saw in all your life! They wear cloth of gold so dazzling that my eyes are still dim with the sight of it. O sir, this is your lucky day! You have but to spur Rosinante towards the road, and you shall see them yourself before you can say "windmills"!'

'Now, Sancho,' said Quixote, 'if you are deceiving me, I shall be so angry with you that you will be sorry that ever you were born.'

'O sir,' answered Sancho, 'fancy saying that! What makes your honour think I would play a trick like that?'

'On the other hand,' said Quixote, 'if you are right, then I shall reward you with all the spoils of our next adventure.'

'Well, never mind about that now,' said Sancho. 'There's no time to lose. Come now—and you shall see what you shall see.'

Without further speech Quixote followed Sancho, and

there before them, on the road that crossed the open fields, they beheld the three country wenches on their dusty asses.

Quixote gazed with troubled eyes towards the town and said in bewildered tones:

'Where is the princess, Sancho? Had she left the town when you spoke to me?'

'But your worship!' said Sancho in a voice of the utmost astonishment. 'Are your worship's eyes in the back of your head? Can you not see the princess and her two damsels coming straight towards you?'

'I see nothing but three country lasses on three donkeys,' answered Quixote.

'Country lasses! Donkeys!' said Sancho. 'Why, these are fine—what d'you call 'em—ambling nags, as fine as ever I saw! How can you call such milk-white steeds donkeys, by my beard? Don't sit there like an idiot, but go and pay homage to the queen of your soul! Why, I never saw such beauty in all my life!'

With these words Sancho jumped off his ass and ran towards the three girls. Then, seizing the halter of one of their donkeys, he fell upon his knees and cried:

'O flower of maidens, I beg you to receive the humble respects of my master, Don Quixote, the knight of la Mancha, who comes to lay himself at your highness's feet. I am his squire, and as you see, he is overcome with amazement to behold the beauty of your high and mightiness.'

Don Quixote, who by this time was kneeling beside Sancho, was indeed struck dumb, but not for the reason Sancho had given. For what he saw in front of him was a more than usually homely girl with something of a squint, greasy black hair and a figure which, while strong and well-built, was by no means graceful. All the girls were astonished to see the two ill-assorted men on their knees in the road. The so-called princess at last spoke.

'Get out of the light, you two clowns,' she said, 'and let us be on our way!'

'O high and mighty princess,' continued Sancho, 'will your highness not open her heart to my unfortunate master who sighs night and day for her favour? Do you not see him prostrate in the dust at your feet? Have pity on him, I beseech, and vouchsafe him one smile from your shapely mouth, one glance from your utterly starlike and never-to-be-forgotten eyes. O universal princess and flower of damsels, look with pity upon your speechless adorer!'

It was now the turn of one of the girls to speak.

'You're nothing but a couple of broken-down gentry come to make fun of us poor girls. Get out of our way, sirs, and let us be about our business!'

'Rise, Sancho!' said Quixote, finding his voice at last. 'I am now convinced that the stars are against me. O matchless Dulcinea, hope of knighthood and pattern of all maidenly virtues, though a spiteful magician persecutes me and hides thy beauty from my sight, under the disguise of rustic deformity, if he has not changed thy faithful knight, the renowned Don Quixote of la Mancha, into some beast as ugly and repulsive as you appear to me, look on me with a loving eye and accept the homage I pay to your beauty, transformed though it is under a hideous cloud!'

'Twaddle!' said the girl. 'Spare your breath to cool your broth, and get out of the way!'

Sancho got up and made way for her to pass, delighted that his plan had been so successful. The imaginary Dulcinea, thoroughly angered by the knight's unwelcome attentions, dug her heels into her donkey and made off as fast as its four legs would carry her. The donkey, not used to such violence, kicked up its heels and threw her. Don Quixote, horrified at this accident to the lady he took to be his princess, ran to her aid, while Sancho attended to the donkey's saddle, which had slipped down under its belly. Quixote attempted to take the girl in his arms and lift her back into the saddle, but she escaped his embrace and jumped on to the donkey's back without assistance.

'My word!' exclaimed Sancho. 'The peerless Dulcinea can hop on to a horse like a bullfighter. And her damsels are no less nimble.'

The two girls had followed the supposed princess, and all three made haste to get as far away from Quixote and his squire as they could.

Don Quixote watched the girls disappear in the distance, and with a sorrowful air he turned to Sancho and said:

'Ah Sancho, am I not the most unfortunate knight alive? How can I escape the malice of the wicked enchanters who persist in thwarting all my hopes? If only I could have seen my lady in her true shape, how eternally blessed I should have been!'

'Indeed, you are right, sir,' answered Sancho. 'But, as the proverb has it, better luck next time!'

— 15 —
The Chariot of Death

Don Quixote rode on in a state of deep melancholy. He was pained and puzzled by the malice of his invisible enemies, the enchanters who had bewitched his lady Dulcinea.

'Was ever a knight so unlucky?' he said to himself. 'Do I not spend all my days and nights thinking of how I can serve my lady? And then, when at last I behold her, she is so enchanted as to be foul and ugly to my sight.'

In this abstracted mood, he gave Rosinante his head, and the prudent horse, seeing some long and luxuriant grass by the wayside, was soon cropping busily.

Sancho, seeing that they were making no progress, and observing his master's downcast countenance, rode up to him and said:

'Sir, what ails you? This is no way to go on. Though I've nicknamed you "the Knight of the Sorrowful

Visage", I never expected to see your worship quite so down in the dumps. This is not the behaviour of a knight errant! Cheer up, sir, and forget about your troubles. Why, all the Madam Dulcineas in Spain aren't worth all this misery!'

At the mention of Dulcinea, Don Quixote raised his head and addressed Sancho with spirit:

'Come, friend,' he said, 'that is no way to talk. Speak no ill of the sweet princess of my heart, for all her misfortunes may be blamed upon me. Were it nor for the malice of my enemies, she would not have been transformed into a plain country wench. Yet I believe her transformation is reserved for my eyes alone. Ah, what it must be to have seen her beauty as it really is!'

'Yes indeed, sir,' agreed Sancho. 'If only you could have seen her hair—tresses, I should say—like gold and her eyes like pearls, as *I* saw them. You'd never forget it, sir—by my beard, you wouldn't!'

'You are indeed privileged,' said Quixote sadly. 'Yet, are you not a little confused, my friend? Your description of her eyes, which you say are like pearls, would be more suitable to a whiting or a cod. You were thinking of her teeth, no doubt, and you should say that her eyes are like emeralds or sapphires.'

'Well, that's as may be, your honour,' replied Sancho. 'My mind *was* a little confused by the lady's beauty. But there's something that worries me. Suppose you meet and conquer a knight or a giant, and send him to pay homage to the lady, how is he going to know her if she's transformed?'

'I dare say,' answered Quixote, 'that she's only transformed to *my* sight, and that her ugliness is reserved for me alone. But let us make proof of it. Next time I see a wandering knight, I will force him to his knees and then make him journey to Toboso, where he must kiss the ground at the feet of my lady. Then he must return to me and report on her appearance. By this means I shall know whether other men see her as I do.'

'An excellent plan, sir,' said Sancho. 'Let's ride on and see if we can find another knight errant.'

At this moment a mule-wagon appeared and was driven across the road. It was an open cart, being in fact a travelling stage, so that Quixote could see everything it contained. The man who drove it was a hideous creature, and other strange figures appeared behind him. The first looked like Death itself with a human face; beside him was an angel with wings of many colours; on the other side of Death was an emperor wearing what seemed to be a golden crown; at the foot of Death lay Cupid, with his bow and his quiver of arrows; there was also a knight, fully armed except for his head, on which he wore a hat adorned with big coloured plumes, as well as several other persons in various strange costumes.

Sancho was scared out of his wits, and Quixote himself was amazed at this odd company. But presently he plucked up resolution.

'Aha!' said he to himself. 'This looks like an adventure, reserved especially for me, to test my courage and my enterprise.'

He rode up to the cart and placed himself squarely in the road in front of it.

'Ho, you carter or coachman or whoever you may be!' he cried. 'Tell me at once who you are, whence you come, and whither you are going.'

'Sir,' answered the driver politely, 'we are a company of strolling actors. This morning we acted a tragedy called "The Parliament of Death" in a town behind the mountains. This afternoon we are to play it again in the town we're just coming to. We didn't trouble to change our clothes, as we haven't far to go. That young man acts the part of Death. That other is an angel; this woman plays the Queen; there is one acts a soldier; he next to him is the Emperor, and I myself play Satan, or the Devil, which is the best part in the play. Is there anything else you'd like to know?'

'Well, I could have sworn there was an adventure here, for I suspected enchantment,' answered Quixote, 'but I can see we mustn't be deceived by appearances. Drive on, sir, and may I wish success to your play? If there is anything I can do for you, I am at your service. When I was a boy I loved plays and dramatic shows, and I would gladly help a travelling company of actors.'

The driver was about to urge his mules forward when there occurred an unlucky accident. One of the company who played the part of the clown had jumped down from the cart and was frisking about in the road. As was the custom of clowns, he had a stick on which were tied three bladders, and his costume was decorated with jingling bells. He pranced about in front of the patient Rosinante, bouncing the bladders up and down. At this Rosinante took fright and trotted away at speed, despite his master's urgent attempts to hold him back. Sancho, seeing Don Quixote's plight, and fearing some accident, immediately got off his ass and went to the knight's assistance. The clown at once jumped on the ass and dug his heels into its sides. Then, beating the animal with his bladders and laughing with glee, he made off in the direction of the town. Just then Rosinante's caper ended in the usual manner. He tripped on a loose stone, so that both horse

and rider went sprawling on the ground. Sancho was in an agony of doubt as to whether to go to the help of his master or his donkey. Loyalty to the knight prevailed, and he hurried to assist Don Quixote to his feet.

Meanwhile the cart had proceeded some distance towards the town.

'O sir,' cried Sancho, as he helped Quixote into the saddle, 'the clown has run off with Dapple.'

'Has he?' cried Quixote. 'Then he shall pay for this! Come, Sancho, follow me. We will easily overtake them and be revenged on the whole company for this insult.'

Then Sancho saw that the clown had jumped off the ass and was following the cart on foot. The ass, glad to be rid of his noisy burden, was trotting back along the road towards his master.

'You needn't trouble yourself, sir,' said Sancho. 'Here's my beast, come back of his own accord and none the worse for wear.'

'Nevertheless,' said Quixote sternly, 'this ruffian must be taught a lesson. I shall take revenge upon some of the clown's companions, even if the emperor himself is among them.'

'O your worship,' begged Sancho, 'please let them alone and don't meddle with them. Anyone who meddles with strolling players will surely come to some harm, for the players are loved wherever they go. They're allowed to fool about, your worship, and nobody minds. If we attack them, you can be sure some of their friends will attack us.'

'I care not,' cried Quixote, 'though all mankind should be their friends. That clown shall never molest my squire's ass unpunished; otherwise he will boast wherever he goes that he scored a victory over the renowned Don Quixote.'

He then set spurs to Rosinante and rode towards the cart, which was by now approaching the town. Sancho hurried up behind him.

'Halt!' roared Quixote as loudly as he could. 'Halt, you villains, and see how I shall punish those who have made sport with an ass which has the task of carrying so honourable a burden as the squire to a knight errant!'

When these words reached the ears of the driver, he stopped, and some of the company dismounted from the cart and stood ready to receive their attackers. Death himself led the defence. The angel and the emperor, and even the Queen and Cupid, ranged themselves behind him, armed with stones from the road. Then with hands uplifted they awaited the arrival of Quixote. The knight, seeing his adversaries drawn up in battle array, halted, in order to consider how best he might attack such a formidable battalion.

Sancho now came up to Quixote and said:

'Sir, I beseech you not to attack these people. They've all got stones, and there's no defence for you unless you can charge them under cover of a brass bell! What chance has one knight against an army—especially when Death himself is in their ranks, and angels and emperors fight with them!'

'Sancho,' answered the knight, 'these men are only players. They said so themselves. They are no more than ordinary men dressed up like Death and the rest. Out of my way, and let me charge them!'

'All the more reason why a knight errant should leave them alone,' answered Sancho cunningly. 'Have you not yourself said a hundred times that you can't attack anyone below the rank of a knight?'

'True,' agreed Quixote. 'You are right to remind me of what I had forgotten. These men are unfit to fight with me. Therefore, Sancho, *you* attack them—go on!'

'No fear, your honour,' said Sancho. 'What chance would *I* have?'

'It is your duty,' said Quixote, 'to avenge the insult offered to your steed. Be of good courage, Sancho. Charge upon the miscreants!'

'Sir,' said Sancho, 'I freely forgive them, and so does poor Dapple. I'm a peaceful fellow with a wife and children. I'm not going to risk a stone in the eye for the honour of my ass! Besides, it's not Christian, sir, if you ask me. It's my duty to forgive and forget.'

'Very well, Sancho,' said Quixote in a tone of disappointment, 'if that is how you feel, I've no more to say. Let us leave these idle players and seek some more worthy adventure.'

With this Sancho heartily agreed. Master and squire turned their steeds and rode off. The players, dropping their stones, climbed once more into the cart. The driver urged his mules on towards the town, and they were soon lost in a cloud of dust.

So ended the adventure of the Chariot of Death, which might have turned out less happily if it had not been for the excellent advice which Sancho Panza gave his master.

— 16 —

The Knight of the Mirrors

When night came on, Quixote and his squire found themselves in a wood, where they determined to pass the hours of darkness. Quixote lay down under an oak and Sancho under a cork tree. Still thinking sadly of the enchantment which had befallen his lady, the knight sank into a doze; while Sancho, thinking of nothing except the question of where his next meal was coming from, was soon snoring comfortably.

Before long two more riders approached very near, and Quixote, aroused from his dreams, heard one of them slide to the ground from his horse and begin a doleful lamentation. By the clanking of his armour Quixote knew him to be another knight; and the second rider, whom he could hear but not see, he took to be his squire.

Quixote found his way softly to Sancho's side under the cork tree and awoke him.

149

'Yonder, if I mistake not,' he said, 'is a knight errant with his squire. This may be some adventure.'

'What sort of adventure?' asked Sancho drowsily.

'I cannot tell. Let us listen to what this melancholy knight is saying.'

The Knight of the Wood, as we may call him, was bemoaning the cruelty of some lady or other, alternately praising her beauty and cursing her hard-heartedness. Then he stopped for a moment, and the listeners heard the sound of some stringed instrument being tuned.

'He must be in love,' said Sancho.

'Naturally,' answered Quixote. 'All knights errant are in love. But hark! I believe he is going to sing.'

The Knight of the Wood now coughed and cleared his throat; then, striking a few chords on his lute, he began as follows:

> Ah cruel fair one, deign to hear
> The pleading of thy lover's lute.
> Come hither and incline thy gracious ear
> To his unhappy suit.
> Fa la la la!
>
> How sweet, how loud the mournful tones
> Of yon bereavèd turtle-dove,
> But none more loudly or more sweetly moans
> Than thy devoted love.
> Fa la la la!

At the end of this ditty the Knight of the Wood heaved a long and profound sigh.

'Poor chap,' said Sancho Panza. 'How he suffers.'

'Ah me!' continued the unhappy lover. 'How hard is thy heart, O lady Casildea of Vandalia! How grievously dost thou torment thy unhappy knight! Though thine eyes be as bright as yonder stars, yet thy ingratitude is as black as the darkness which surrounds me in this be-nighted grove. What more can I do to prove my devotion? Is it not enough that I have made thee to be acknowledged peerless by all the knights in Navarre, in Leon, in Castille, and even in la Mancha?'

'The man is talking nonsense,' said Don Quixote to Sancho. 'He must be mad to talk like that of the knights of la Mancha.'

'Who's there?' called the Knight of the Wood, on hearing the voice of Quixote. 'Tell me, stranger, are you of the happy sort of men or the miserable?'

'I am of the miserable sort,' answered Quixote.

'Come here, then,' said the other knight, 'and look upon misery itself. I am the most miserable knight alive, and you too, I take it, are a knight errant like myself.'

'Indeed yes,' replied Don Quixote. 'I too am a wander-ing knight, and I shall be glad to lend an ear to your afflictions.'

'Are you in love?' asked the Knight of the Wood. 'And is your lady cruel and heartless, as mine is?'

'I am in love,' said Quixote, 'but at present I do not suffer as you do.'

'I can feel nothing but scorn and hatred for one who can treat me as my lady Casildea does,' said the Knight of the Wood.

'My master doesn't feel that way,' said Sancho. 'The lady Dulcinea is as mild and gentle as a lamb.'

'Is that your squire?' asked the Knight of the Wood. 'I am surprised that any knight should permit his squire to interrupt him while he is in conversation with a fellow knight.'

'I talk when I like,' answered Sancho. 'My master

hasn't found anything against it in the rules of chivalry.'

'My squire,' said the Knight of the Wood, 'never interrupts me.'

'So you're this gentleman's squire,' said Sancho, peering through the darkness at the figure of the other rider. 'Come over here and let's have a talk. I love talking, but I don't want to push myself in where I'm not wanted.'

So Don Quixote and the other knight remained side by side, while the two squires went some distance away to a little glade, where they sat down against the trunk of a great oak and began chatting as if they had been old friends.

'What do you think of this wandering life?' asked the Squire of the Wood. 'It's a troublesome business, and we certainly earn our living by the sweat of our brows, as you might say.'

'It might be worse,' said Sancho. 'The only thing that's wrong with it is that we never know when we're going to get a square meal. Still, one day I shall get the island I've been promised, I've no doubt, and that'll make up for everything.'

'H'm!' said the other squire. 'These islands can be more nuisance than they're worth. I tell you what, my friend—why don't we jog along home together and leave our masters to look after themselves? What's better than a bit of hunting and fishing in our own country?'

'You're right there,' agreed Sancho. 'My master's mad, you know—completely potty, if you ask me.'

'So's mine,' said the Squire of the Wood. 'At least, he's in love, and that's the same thing. Very poor company he is. For two pins I'd leave him and go my own way. What do you say?'

Sancho thought for a moment and then said:

'I don't think I could do that. You see, it's being so crazy that makes him need me. He does all the good he can and hurts nobody. He's as foolish as an old cracked pitcher, and he's so simple that a child could tell him it was the middle of the night when it was broad daylight, and he'd believe it. But he's honest and hasn't a grain of wickedness in him; and he's so simple I couldn't possibly leave him. He needs looking after, you know.'

'I see,' said the Squire of the Wood. 'Well, my master's not like that. But you sound a bit dry in the throat to me. How about a drop to drink and a bite to eat?'

'Well now,' said Sancho readily, 'I shouldn't mind that at all, for I've nothing left myself but a piece of stale bread and a lump of cheese that's like a rock.'

The other squire fetched a wine-skin and a great pie from his saddle-bag; and without having to be asked twice, Sancho lost no time in eating and drinking his fill.

'That's a very nice drop of wine, my friend,' he said. 'If you can get food and drink like this, you don't do so badly.'

They talked on into the night, and when all the provisions had gone, they both felt drowsy; so bidding one another good night, they went to sleep.

The two knights, meanwhile, were talking no less freely. But it was not of food and drink they spoke but of knight errantry, of the great heroes of old, of battles and combats with dragons. But the Knight of the Wood could not long keep off the subject with which his mind was filled—the story of his unhappy devotion to the hard-hearted Casildea of Vandalia.

'She is a tyrant,' he groaned, 'a fiend in the shape of an angel. She makes me perform task after task, like the twelve labours of Hercules; and when each is finished, does she reward me for my services? No, she devises other tasks more fearful and troublesome than all the others. Why, first she made me fight the giantess, Giralda of Seville. No sooner had I done this than she told me to raise from their bases the huge and massive statues of the Bulls of Guisando. They are carved of solid stone, and I thought I should have died in the attempt.'

'And did your lady not reward this feat with a smile and a word of praise?' asked Quixote.

'She did not,' said the Knight of the Woods sadly. 'She made me go instantly and descend into the cave of Cabra and bring her an account of the wonders I beheld there. I descended into this grisly cavern, full of perils and monsters, where I was within an inch of losing my life.'

'And what then?' asked Quixote.

'She did but devise a new task. She made me travel through the entire land of Spain, making all the knights errant I meet acknowledge her beauty. So for the past six months I have fought with knights over the length and breadth of the country. Wherever I found one who would not admit that my lady is the flower of all ladies in Christendom, I have brought him to his knees and made him pay homage to her. Many and fierce are the heroes and the cavaliers I have overcome in her service. I could tell you the names of a hundred famous warriors with whom I have fought. I will only say that my greatest triumph of all was to vanquish the renowned and never-to-be-sufficiently-honoured Don Quixote, knight of la Mancha and foremost of the heroes of these times.'

At this Don Quixote was so amazed that he could scarcely restrain his anger. He almost smote the Knight of the Wood for his lying boast. But in hopes of finding out whether the knight was mad or only lying, he spoke quietly and peaceably.

'Surely, sir knight,' he said, 'you are mistaken. How can you be sure it was indeed Don Quixote you overcame? What was he like?'

'He was tall and withered,' answered the Knight of the Wood. 'He was a lean, scraggy, grey-haired, hawk-nosed fellow; and he had for squire one Sancho Panza, a labouring man who rode upon a donkey. He himself bestrode the famous charger Rosinante. He was sworn to the service of a lady called Dulcinea from Toboso.'

'Sir,' answered Quixote, 'I find it hard to believe your story.'

'If you do not,' cried the other knight, 'here is my sword to prove it.'

'Don Quixote is my friend,' said Quixote, 'and I may

155

say that I know him as well as I know myself. The description you have given of him is accurate in every detail. But I beg leave to suggest, sir, that it was not Quixote himself you overcame but his enemy, an enchanter who can transform himself into the likeness of Don Quixote for his own evil purposes. Why, only two days ago this foul wizard changed the peerless Dulcinea into a plain country wench.'

'Sir,' said the Knight of the Wood hotly, 'I tell you, the man I overcame was Don Quixote himself!'

'And I say,' cried Quixote, 'that it was not! Here is my sword to prove it. For the man you have been speaking of is none other than myself, Don Quixote, knight of la Mancha and servant to the lady Dulcinea, fairest and most virtuous of ladies!'

'If that is what you say,' answered the other, 'there is only one thing to be done. We must fight. As soon as dawn comes, I shall require you to answer my challenge with your life!'

'Right gladly!' said Quixote. 'For let no false knight boast that he overcame me, so long as I have breath to deny it and strength to prove him a villain.'

'We fight at dawn then, and he that is winner shall have the loser absolutely at his mercy, to do what he likes with. Is that agreed?'

'Agreed,' said Quixote, 'only provided that he asks him to do nothing unworthy of his place amongst the order of knighthood.'

So the two knights prepared to fight at dawn. They went and roused their squires and told them to make ready their horses. Sancho was worried as to what might happen to his master, for he had heard during the night many tales of the courage and fury of Quixote's adversary.

'I tell you what,' said the other squire; 'we may have to do a bit of fighting ourselves, you and I.'

'By no means,' said Sancho, 'there's nothing in the rules of knighthood to say that squires must fight when their masters do. Besides, I haven't got a sword.'

'That's easily remedied,' said the Squire of the Wood. 'I've two linen bags with me. We can bang each other with those.'

'Oh, if you want a pillow-fight,' said Sancho, 'that suits me all right.'

'We'll put a few smooth stones in the bags,' said the other squire, 'and make it more like a real battle.'

'Certainly not,' answered Sancho. 'I don't like banging a man with stones in cold blood—especially a man I've shared food and drink with. I'll have nothing to do with it.'

By this time the birds had begun to sing melodiously in the branches, and the sun at last appeared in the eastern sky. Then Sancho and his master saw for the first time the men they had been talking with. The first thing that Sancho saw was his companion's nose. It was the largest nose he had ever seen on any human being. It was red and covered with knobs, and it hung down over his mouth, almost to his chin. Sancho was terrified at the sight of such a nose.

Quixote saw that the man he was to fight was short, well-built and of nimble appearance. His face was hidden by his visor, and over his armour he wore a doublet on which were sewn pieces of mirror shaped like half-moons, on which the rising sun gleamed brightly.

'Sir Knight of the Mirrors,' cried Quixote, 'you are of goodly appearance. But show me your face, I pray, that I may see whether you are as handsome as you seem.'

157

'There will be time enough for that later,' answered the Knight of the Mirrors.

'Then tell me whether I am like that Quixote whom you say you overcame.'

'You are indeed. But let us fight, so that we may prove whether or not it was some enchantment or the very knight himself that I vanquished.'

So the two warriors rode apart. When they had separated some distance, both wheeled in order to charge upon the other. Then Quixote caught sight of the nose on the face of his enemy's squire, and at the same time Sancho ran towards him and laid hold of his bridle.

'Help me into this tree, master!' he cried. 'I am terrified of this fellow with the great nose; and if you should be killed in this fight, I will be left to deal with him alone.'

'I can well understand,' answered Quixote, 'that any man except me might be scared of a face like that, so I will do as you say and help you into a tree.'

When he had done this, he set spurs to Rosinante and charged upon his foe. The horse, for once and once only in the whole of this story, almost galloped; so with great fury, his lance quivering before him, Quixote dashed towards the Knight of the Mirrors. That unfortunate gentleman, seeing Quixote engaged with his squire, had checked his horse and was now unable to get him to move again. He became at the same time so mixed up with his lance, which was an unusually long and heavy one, that he was quite helpless to withstand the furious onslaught of his opponent. Thus Quixote was able without difficulty to unseat him, and the Knight of the Mirrors was thrown right over his horse's head and fell senseless and unarmed to the ground.

Instantly Quixote leaped from his saddle and knelt at the knight's head, unlacing his helmet and raising the visor. What was his astonishment to behold, pale and motionless, the face of his old friend Samson Carrasco, the scholar from Salamanca.

Sancho Panza, seeing his master's victory, had made a speedy descent from his tree and now stood by Quixote's side, gazing at the seemingly lifeless face of Samson.

'Aha!' he said. 'This is evidently your enemy the enchanter who has transformed himself into the likeness of Samson Carrasco. Kill him instantly, I beg you, for now your worst enemy is at your mercy.'

'There is something in what you say, Sancho,' said Quixote. 'I will show the foul wizard no mercy!'

So saying, he raised his sword and was about to cut off his opponent's head when the Squire of the Mirrors came running up. He no longer had his enormous nose.

'Hold, sir!' he cried. 'Don't kill my master. It's only Samson Carrasco, the scholar. He's no enchanter! Don't kill him, I implore you.'

'What have you done with your nose?' asked Sancho.

'It's here in my pocket,' answered the squire, pulling out a cardboard nose and showing it to the astonished Sancho. 'I joined Samson Carrasco on his quest, and in order not to be recognized, I wore this nose.'

'By the hairs of my beard!' cried Sancho, gazing hard on the Squire of the Mirrors. 'It's Thomas, my old friend from la Mancha!'

'It is indeed,' said Thomas, 'your old friend and neighbour. I'll tell you all about how this happened later.'

By this time Samson Carrasco had recovered somewhat and was sitting up rubbing his bruises.

'Now,' said Quixote sternly, 'admit that you did not overcome the famous Don Quixote, and that his lady Dulcinea of Toboso is the flower of flowers, peerless among ladies; promise that you will journey forthwith to Toboso to lay yourself at her feet and ask her pardon for having doubted the faith of her true knight. Then return to me and tell me what passed between you, giving an account of her appearance and of her manner of speech.'

'I will, I will,' answered Samson. 'I acknowledge all this, and I promise to do as you have said.'

To make a long story short, Quixote and Sancho took leave of the others and rode off in the direction of Saragossa. Samson Carrasco picked himself up painfully and remounted his horse. Then calling to Thomas to follow him, he went off in search of the nearest town where he might get ointment for his bruises.

Now the reason why Samson and his squire had pursued Quixote in disguise was that a plot had been hatched between the scholar and the priest and barber of Quixote's village. Seeing that the knight would never willingly be cured of his folly, they persuaded Samson to go in search of Quixote and make him fight, for they thought that Quixote would be easily beaten. Then Samson would force him to return home and stay there for at least two years, by which time they hoped he would give up his mad notions and agree to lead a more homely life.

'Well, sir,' said Thomas, as they jogged along towards the town, 'we seem to have got the worst of the bargain. You and I are in our right minds, and Don Quixote is mad; but it's he who has won the battle and is probably laughing at us both at this very moment. Come, sir, let's get home as fast as we can and tell them what's happened.'

'You may go home,' answered Samson Carrasco, 'but I—as soon as I have recovered from my fall—I shall look round for some means of revenging myself upon this crazy but redoubtable knight.'

— 17 —
The Adventure of the Lions

As Don Quixote and his squire were jogging along the road, a gentleman in green overtook them, riding a mare. He wished them good day very civilly and had soon passed them. But Don Quixote called after him:

'Sir, if you are not in too much of a hurry, ride with us, I beg you, for so long as we travel the same road.'

Hearing this, the gentleman reined in his mare and turned round to look at the knight. Quixote presented a strange figure, for although he was without his helmet, which Sancho carried slung beside Dapple, his rusty armour, his sword and lance, his bony horse and, above all, his own thin and care-worn visage were not at all what would be seen every day upon the road. Quixote in turn looked at the gentleman in green, who appeared to be a well-to-do country squire.

The two stood for some time in conversation. Quixote

told the gentleman that he was a famous hero who had given up everything to revive the ancient glory of knight errantry.

'I am,' he said, 'the champion of the widow and the poor, the enemy of cruelty and cowardice. Sometimes I plunge headlong to disaster, but afterwards I rise and perform feats of valour which have earned me great fame.'

The gentleman in green said he was astonished that there should still be one living who practised the ancient calling of knight errant.

'As for me,' he said, 'I do not go out looking for adventures. I stay peaceably at home. I manage my estate, which is not far from here, and do what good I can to the poorer people round about. I relieve their distresses and settle their quarrels. I am a man of peace, and I like nothing so much as to go hunting and fishing. Yet I keep neither hawk nor hound myself, but only some tame partridges and a ferret. I have a few score books in my library, but none of them are books of knight errantry. I confess that I have little use for old-fashioned books of romance which, in my opinion, are nothing but lies and rubbish.'

At this Quixote was somewhat indignant, and a long and interesting discussion took place about the truth or falsehood of the tales of olden days.

Sancho had little interest in talk of this kind, and had strayed off the road to speak with some shepherds who were minding their sheep not far away. He noticed that they had a quantity of cheese—or rather, thick sour milk called curds, which would have turned into cream cheese if it had been kept a little longer. He bargained with the shepherds for some of the curds, and had just paid for it when he heard his master calling him.

In the midst of his conversation with the gentleman in green Quixote saw a wagon approaching. It was drawn by two mules, on one of which sat the driver. Another man was sitting idly on the front part of the wagon, and on it were mounted a number of little flags, which showed that it was being used in the service of some important person.

'Aha!' cried Quixote. 'This looks like an adventure. Sancho! Where are you, Sancho? Bring me my helmet at once!'

Sancho had at that very moment paid for the curds and, being unwilling to lose them, looked round for something to put them in. All he could find was his master's helmet. So dropping the curds hastily into it, he dug his heels into his ass and had soon reached Quixote's side.

Then a dreadful event occurred. Snatching the helmet from his squire, the knight clapped it firmly on his head without stopping to look inside it. Instantly the curds ran down over his hair and face, and dripped on to his beard.

'Mercy on us!' cried Quixote. 'Do my brains become soft, and has my skull been cracked open? Or do I sweat? If so, it is not for fear, though I dare swear that this will be a very terrible adventure.'

He took off the helmet and ordered Sancho to give him something with which to wipe the mess from his face. Sancho gave him a cloth, and the knight, after wiping his face, put the cloth to his nose.

'What is this?' he said. 'It smells like curds. Villain and traitor! Have you been putting curds in my helmet?'

'O sir,' said Sancho reproachfully, 'do you think I, your faithful squire, would do a thing like that? Where should I get curds from? And if I had any, would I not

rather put them in my mouth than your helmet? Now by
my beard, this is the work of some enchanter. I dare say
I have an invisible enemy, just like your worship has, and
he wants to set your worship against me for following
you and being your squire.'

'There may be something in that,' agreed Quixote.

The gentleman in green, meanwhile, stood by, astonished at what was going on. He was still more astonished
to see the knight replace the helmet on his head, test his
sword to see if it was loose in the scabbard, place his lance
in the rest, and adopt a challenging and war-like attitude.

By this time the wagon had come up close, and Quixote
called out:

'Whither go you, friends? What wagon is this? What
do you carry in it, and what is the meaning of these
colours?'

'The wagon is mine,' answered the driver. 'Inside it
are two brave lions which a general in Africa has sent to
the King of Spain. These colours are to let everyone

know that this wagon is loaded with the King's property.'

'Are the lions large?' asked Quixote.

'Very large,' said the man on the front of the wagon. 'There never came bigger lions from Africa into Spain. I am their keeper and have had charge of many others. But I never saw the like of these before. In the front cage is a he-lion, and in the other a lioness. By this time they're in a raging hunger, for they've eaten nothing all day. Therefore, good sir, ride out of the way and let us pass, for we must hurry to get to the place where we mean to feed them.'

'What!' cried Quixote. 'A couple of paltry lions sent against *me*, Don Quixote of la Mancha? Do you think I am scared of such puny beasts? I have fought giants and dragons and am not to be scared by creatures like these. Get down at once, friend keeper, and open the doors of their cages. *I* will show them what it is to encounter Don Quixote of la Mancha!'

The gentleman in green was beginning to wonder if the curds which had been put in Quixote's helmet had indeed softened his brain, when Sancho hurried up to him and begged him to stop his master.

'O dear sir,' said the squire in fear and trembling, 'don't let my master attack these frightful animals, or we shall all be torn to pieces.'

'Is your master mad then?' asked the gentleman. 'Will he really set on the lions?'

'He is not mad but rash,' answered Sancho.

'I'll soon stop him,' said the gentleman, and rode up to Quixote, who was trying to get the keeper to release the lions.

'Sir,' said he earnestly, 'I beg you not to undertake this adventure, but to go in search of tasks worthy of the attention of a knight errant. These lions are not sent against you—they are a present to the King, and it would be foolish to meddle with them. It is not bravery but foolhardiness to attack wild beasts.'

'Kind sir,' said Quixote haughtily, 'go home and play with your tame partridges and your ferret. I know my own business best and whether or not these paltry lions are sent against me.'

He then turned to the keeper and said in threatening tones:

'You rogue,' he said, 'open your cages immediately or I will pin you to your wagon with this lance and open them myself!'

The wagoner, terrified at the strange appearance of the knight in armour, cried out:

'Sir, if you intend to let the lions out, at least give me time to unharness my mules and take them to a safe place. My wagon and mules are all I have in the world, and if the lions get at them they'll tear them to pieces.'

'Very well,' said Quixote, 'since you have no faith in the power of my arm, take away your mules, coward that you are, and you shall presently see that your precautions are needless. Do you think that the world-famous knight of la Mancha is no match for two ordinary lions?'

'Now,' said the keeper, 'let everyone get as far away as he can while I open the cages. This gentleman gives me no choice in the matter, but I call you all to witness that he is responsible for all the damage the lions will do. They won't hurt me, for they know their keeper, but I won't answer for anyone else.'

'I beg you,' said the gentleman to Quixote, 'not to do this mad and foolhardy thing. Consider your own safety, I implore you.'

'I know what I have to do,' answered Quixote resolutely. 'If you are afraid, set spurs to your mare and get out of harm's way. I have man's work to do!'

'O master,' said Sancho, with tears in his eyes, 'do give up this madness, I beg! This is worse than the windmills, and the fulling-mills, and all your other adventures put together. There's no enchantment here, I swear. I peeped between the bars of the cage just now and saw a claw—a real, live lion's claw; and the lion on the other end of that claw must be a fearsome monster. O sir, don't do it for pity's sake!'

'You are afraid,' answered Quixote, 'and your fear makes the lion seem far bigger than he is. Be not alarmed for my sake. Come on, you!' he said to the keeper. 'Why haven't you opened that door yet?'

The gentleman in green, seeing that it was no use trying to interfere with a madman, galloped away on his mare; Sancho with Dapple, and the driver with his mules followed after him as fast as they could go. Poor Sancho moaned and lamented, for he was sure he would never again see his master alive.

'O dear,' he told himself, 'now he's really gone and done it. He hasn't a hope this time, poor fellow!'

When the others had gone a safe distance, the keeper once more entreated Quixote not to make him open the cage, but Quixote would not listen to him. Instead he stood wondering whether to meet the lions on horseback or to descend to the ground and fight them on foot. He decided that since Rosinante was not used to lions, he might take fright. Accordingly he dismounted, threw aside his lance, held his shield in front of him and grasped his sword firmly in his right hand. Then he placed himself directly before the door of the foremost cage and he commended himself first to Heaven and then to his lady Dulcinea.

The keeper, seeing that Quixote was desperate and that it was useless to argue any longer, opened the door of the cage in which lay the he-lion. The creature was of monstrous size and hideous appearance. The first thing he did was to roll and turn himself round in his cage.

Next, he stretched out one paw, pushed out his claws and roused himself. After that he gaped and yawned, showing his enormous jaws and dreadful teeth. Next, he stuck out half a yard of broad red tongue, and with it licked the dust out of his eyes. Then he stuck his huge head right out of the cage and looked round with his two eyes, which were like burning coals. It was a sight to strike terror to the heart of the boldest. But Quixote only gazed at the monster attentively, hoping fervently that it would leap

169

from the cage and attack him, so that he could destroy it and cut it in pieces. But the lion refused to fulfil Quixote's hopes. It was, despite its ferocious look, a gentle beast, and all it did was to look at Quixote with complete unconcern, turn slowly round, wave its tail lazily at Quixote, and retire once more into its cage.

'Do you see that?' said the knight. 'Force him out of the cage with your pole, and let me get at him.'

'Not I!' said the keeper with determination. 'If I annoy him, I'll be the first he'll tear to pieces. I beseech you, sir, go no further in your folly. You've done a good day's work. No man could do more. The door is open. If the lion wants to come out, he will. You see, he scarcely even looked you in the face; and seeing he hasn't come out yet, I don't suppose he would come out if we stayed like this all day. You've shown quite enough courage, sir. After this, no one could doubt it.'

'True,' said Quixote. 'You are right. Close the door again, for I see I must be satisfied with this proof of my valour.'

The keeper, with profound relief, did as Quixote said. Then the knight sheathed his sword and took up his lance, on whose point he stuck the cloth with which he had wiped the curds from his face. This he waved in the air, and shouted to the rest of the party to return. They were well out of earshot by this time, but Sancho turned and saw the signal of the white flag.

'My master calls to us!' cried Sancho. 'Blow me if he hasn't beaten the lions after all! Let's go back and see what's happened.'

With tears of joy in his eyes the squire hurried back to Don Quixote. The gentleman in green and the wagoner with his mules were not far behind.

'See friends,' cried Quixote, 'how my valour has triumphed! Friend wagoner, harness your mules again; and Sancho, give him and the keeper a ducat apiece, to make up for the time I have delayed them.'

'Willingly,' answered Sancho. 'But what's happened to the lions? Did you do for them, sir?'

Then the keeper told them what had happened, making the most of his story and exaggerating Quixote's heroism to the best of his skill.

'Why, the he-lion took one look at the knight,' he said, 'and skulked back into his cage. The door was left open for longer than I dare to think, but the animal was so terrified he couldn't be got out by any means whatever. This gentleman wanted me to force the creature out, but I persuaded him at last to have mercy on the creature and let me shut the door. I've never seen anything like it in my life!'

'Well, Sancho,' said Quixote, 'what do you think of this? Doesn't it prove that enchantment has no power in the end against truth and fortitude?'

The keeper and the wagoner took their ducats, and the keeper promised to tell the King himself of Don Quixote's noble act as soon as he got to court with the lions.

'Tell the King,' said Quixote, 'that the man who performed this deed was no other than the Knight of the Lions—for that is what I intend to call myself from now on! This was the custom with all knights errant—to change their names as often as they pleased, and so record the memory of their greatest exploits.'

The keeper promised to do as Quixote bade, and presently he and the wagoner made off along the road. The gentleman in green, still marvelling at the extra-

171

ordinary mixture of courage and foolishness which he had just witnessed, invited the knight and his squire to accompany him to his house.

'Come,' he said, 'it grows late, and no doubt you are in need of rest and refreshment. If you will deign to accept the hospitality of a peace-loving gentleman like myself, I shall be happy to entertain you.'

'Lead on, Sir Knight of the Green Doublet!' answered Quixote. 'It will give me pleasure to honour your castle with my presence.'

— 18 —

The Puppet Show of Master Pedro

Some days later Quixote and his squire were lodged at an inn where was gathered a fair company of guests. One evening a travelling man came in and asked for lodgings.

'Down the road,' said he, 'is the fortune-telling ape and the puppet show of Melisandra's deliverance. They'll be here directly.'

'Why, it's Master Pedro!' exclaimed the landlord, a fat, genial fellow, always out of breath from serving his customers and fetching up wine from the cellar. 'There's good company here tonight that should pay well to see your show. But where's the ape and the puppets? I don't see them.'

'I only came on ahead to see if you had lodgings,' said Master Pedro. 'The cart is down the road with the boy.'

'Why, of course there's always room for you,' answered the landlord. 'Go and fetch the cart as soon as you like.'

Master Pedro was a strong, well-built man with a face weather-beaten through much travelling. He made off as fast as he could, while Don Quixote, who had been listening with interest, inquired about him of the landlord.

'Who is this Master Pedro?' he asked.

'Why, he's a travelling showman,' explained the landlord. 'He goes round the countryside with one of the best puppet shows you ever saw—the play of Melisandra and how she was rescued from a wicked Moor. Then he's got an ape—such an ape as you never saw in your life. It can tell everything that has happened and everything that is likely to happen. Ask it any question you please about what's happened to you any time in your life, and up he jumps on to his master's shoulder and whispers the answer. Then Master Pedro tells you what the ape told him. He charges twopence for every question. That must mount up by the end of the year, and they do say that Pedro has put away a tidy sum. But no one deserves it better. He's as merry a fellow as you'd want to meet— talks like six men, he does, and drinks like twelve.'

By this time Master Pedro had returned with his ape and his puppet show in a cart.

'Sir,' said Quixote, 'will your ape be so good as to tell us what fish we shall catch and what will become of us? Here is your fee. Sancho, give this gentleman twopence.'

'Sir,' answered Pedro, 'my ape can tell you nothing of the future, though he knows a good deal about the past.'

'Oh indeed?' said Sancho. 'I wouldn't give a farthing to know what's happened in the past, for I know it all myself. Still, if he knows what's going on in the present, here's twopence for him to tell me what my wife Teresa's doing now.'

'I won't take your money in advance,' said the

174

showman. 'If you're satisfied, you can pay me after.'

So he clapped himself on the left shoulder, and the ape skipped up and began chattering and grimacing in his master's ear. Then he skipped down on to the ground again.

Instantly Master Pedro knelt at the feet of Don Quixote and, embracing his knees, said:

'O glorious restorer of knight errantry, I embrace these legs as I would the pillars of Hercules. Who can sufficiently praise the great Don Quixote of la Mancha, the raiser of the fallen, the prop and stay of the falling, and the staff of comfort to the weak?'

At this everyone was amazed, not least Don Quixote himself.

'And thou, honest Sancho Panza,' continued the showman, 'the best squire to the best knight in the world—bless thy stars! For thy good wife Teresa is a good housewife and is at this moment spinning flax, with a broken jug full of wine at her left elbow to refresh her spirits.'

'That's likely enough,' said Sancho, 'for she is, as you say, a good worker, and is partial to a drop of wine.'

'I too am amazed at the knowledge displayed by this ape,' said Quixote. 'He has described me exactly, and I am gratified that my reputation should have spread so far.'

Then a young man in the crowd said:

'I should be glad, Master Showman, to know what luck I shall have in the wars, for I am shortly off to join the army.'

'I've told you already,' said Master Pedro, 'my ape knows nothing of what is to come. But now, gentlemen, as a mark of the esteem in which I hold this great and

175

noble knight, Don Quixote, I will set up my show in this inn and give you all a performance free, gratis and for nothing!'

There was loud applause and the landlord, highly delighted with this offer, immediately appointed a room for Master Pedro to set up his show, and the showman and his boy at once went off to arrange things. It was not long before Pedro returned to the company and told them that all was ready. So everyone trooped into a large room at the back of the house, which was lit by wax candles and had benches arranged in rows in front of the showman's booth. Master Pedro went behind to work the puppets, and the boy stayed in front to point with his stick and tell the story that was to be acted.

The assembled company, who were talking excitedly, were silenced by the sound of drums and trumpets from behind the stage. Then, when everyone was quiet, the boy raised his voice and said:

'Ladies and gentlemen, we present you here with a true history taken from the chronicles of France and the ancient ballads of Spain. It tells you how Don Gayferos delivered his wife Melisandra from the Moors in the city of Saragossa. The first scene, ladies and gentlemen, portrays Gayferos at court playing chess, as the ballad relates.

'Now Gayferos the livelong day,
O shameful knight! at chess doth play,
And as at court most husbands do,
Forgets his wife who loves him true.

'Now, fair ladies and gallant cavaliers, do you see that personage peeping out there with a crown on his head and a sceptre in his hand? That is the Emperor

176

Charlemagne, the father of the fair Melisandra. He is angry at his son-in-law's idleness, and comes to reproach him. See how passionately he scolds, as if he would like to hit him a blow or two over the head with his sceptre. ' "You're an idle vagabond!" says the Emperor. "Look to your business. I say no more!" And with that the Emperor departs.'

Here Don Quixote leaned forward with an expression of the utmost concern on his lean and withered countenance. He shook his head gravely as the puppet Don Gayferos rose up from his seat and began pacing angrily to and fro.

'Now see how Don Gayferos,' continued the boy, pointing with his stick, 'throws the chessmen about the room and calls for his armour. Now he borrows his cousin Orlando's sword Durindana. Orlando offers to go along with Gayferos, but the enraged knight says he will go and rescue his wife without the help of anyone. So off he goes, ladies and gentlemen, to put on his armour.

'Now cast your eyes upon that lofty tower. It is part of the castle of Saragossa, and the lady you see there on the balcony is the peerless Melisandra. She is dressed like a Moorish lady, for she is in the power of the Moorish King. She casts her eyes towards France, where her husband is, and wrings her hands to Heaven for comfort.'

At this a murmur of wonder broke out among the audience, and the boy once more raised his voice.

'Silence, I beg you!' he said. 'Here is a marvel, the like of which was never seen before. Do you behold that crafty Moor, tiptoeing and stealing along behind Melisandra? See how he kisses her lips before she can turn and discover him, and see how angrily she spits and wipes her mouth upon her white sleeve! Now look at that grave and serious Moor who stands upon the parapet of the castle. He is Marsilius, King of Saragossa. He has observed the sauciness of the other Moor, whom he orders to be whipped for his familiarity with the lady Melisandra. The sentence is immediately executed, for among the Moors there is no trial, and no process of law.'

'Boy, boy!' interrupted Quixote. 'I tell you there must be a trial before execution can be done. Stick to the story as it happened, I beg you, and do not give us your own inventions.'

'Boy,' said Master Pedro from behind the scenes, 'do as the gentleman says, and get on with the story.'

'I will,' said the boy. 'Now, fair ladies and noble sirs, do but observe that rider wrapped up in his cloak and approaching at the gallop. That is Don Gayferos himself.

Now he is beneath the walls of the tower, and his wife Melisandra, taking him for a stranger, addresses him thus:

> ' "Ah, gracious traveller, if perchance
> You ride afar to fairest France,
> For pity's sake ask when you're there
> For Gayferos, my husband dear."

'And now you may see how he makes himself known to his wife and how, with gestures of joy and delight, she recognizes her husband. See how she lets herself down from the balcony in order to join Gayferos.'

At this everyone in the audience clapped and cheered, but suddenly all were silent, as the boy went on:

'But what accident is this? See, one of the skirts of her dress has caught on a spike of the balcony, and there she hangs in the air without being able to get down. But the gallant Gayferos rescues her from her pitiful situation, lifts her down and sets her astride upon his horse's crupper. Then he mounts behind her. See now how the horse neighs and prances, proud of the burden upon his back. And now they gallop off towards France. Peace be upon the souls of these two true lovers! May you, O faithful pair, get safe and sound to your own country!

'But alas, ladies and gentlemen! the tale is not yet ended. For some of those sneaking busybodies who love to pry into other people's affairs have seen Melisandra's escape. Straightaway they run and tell Marsilius of it. The King sounds an alarm. Heaven bless us! What a din and hurly-burly there is! How the city shakes with the ringing of bells in all the mosques! How——'

'You are wrong, boy!' cried Quixote. 'The Moors have no bells. They only use kettle-drums and trumpets.'

'Now sir,' cried Master Pedro from behind, 'if you

179

make a fuss about every detail, we shall never please you. Get on with the story, boy, and let us have no more interruptions.'

'Now sirs,' proceeded the boy, 'observe what a vast company of horsemen comes pouring out of the city of Saragossa in pursuit of the lovers! What a dreadful sound of trumpets and drums there is in the air! I fear they will overtake them, and then the poor wretches will be captured and treated most barbarously. Ah, what a terrible fate awaits the faithful Gayferos and his wife Melisandra!'

At this Don Quixote could remain silent no longer. His pale face was red with fury, and his whole body was trembling. He rose from his seat on the bench and cried:

'It shall never be said while I live, that I allowed such a wrong to be done to so famous a knight and so daring a lover as Don Gayferos! Give up this unjust pursuit, ye baseborn heathens! Stop instantly, or prepare to face my wrath!'

Without further speech he drew his sword and sprang at the puppet show. Brandishing his weapon, he cut and slashed at the Moorish puppets, hacking at them in a most terrible manner. Some he threw to the ground; others he beheaded. Arms and legs lay all over the stage, heads rolled hither and thither, cloaks and weapons were mingled in confusion. One blow was so ferocious that, had not Master Pedro ducked and squatted down, it would have cut his head from his body.

'Stop it, sir! Stop it at once! These aren't real Moors —they're only made of cardboard. If you don't leave off at once, you'll ruin me for ever!'

But Don Quixote took no notice. In his rage he continued to lay about him with his sword till he had cut all the strings and wires, mangled the puppets and utterly demolished the whole puppet show. King Marsilius was in a grievous state, and the Emperor Charlemagne's head and crown were split in two. The whole audience was in an uproar of dismay and disappointment. The ape in terror ran off to the top of the house, and Sancho cowered in a corner, overcome with fright. He had never before seen his master in such a fury.

Having wrecked the show, Quixote now calmed somewhat. Breathless and triumphant, his sword still in his hand, he turned upon the audience.

'Now, ladies and gentlemen,' he shouted, 'which of you denies any longer the power and glory of knight errantry? Did you not see the plight of those two poor lovers, and the pursuing hordes of heathen Moors? If I had not been there to rescue Don Gayferos and the faithful Melisandra, second only to the peerless Dulcinea, which of you can deny that these barbarians would have recaptured them and treated them with the utmost savagery? Long live Don Gayferos, say I! Long live Melisandra! Long live knight errantry!'

'It's all very well for you,' said Master Pedro miserably, standing among the ruins of his puppet show, 'but what about me? Yesterday I had fine possessions—great kings and emperors at my command—horses and slaves at my bidding. Now I have nothing, and all thanks to this brave knight here, the redresser of wrongs and rescuer of maidens in distress. I have lost everything—and worst of all, I've lost my ape. Goodness knows if I shall ever get *him* back again!'

'Cheer up, Master Pedro,' said Sancho, who was downcast to see the showman's distress. 'My master isn't a hard man. I guarantee that when he comes to see how

181

much harm he has done you, he'll pay for every bit of damage—on my honour he will.'

'Well, if he'll pay me for the puppets he's broken,' said Pedro, 'I'll forgive and forget. If not, Heaven help him.'

'But in what way have I injured you, honest show-man?' asked Quixote.

'Why, bless me, sir!' said Master Pedro. 'Have you not slaughtered all my puppets, and were they not my only support in life? How can I live now that I have none to support me?'

'Ladies and gentlemen,' said Quixote, 'I do swear before you all that what seemed to be going on before my eyes was no puppet show but a true happening. To me Gayferos *was* Gayferos and Melisandra *was* Melisandra. I believed every word of the tale just as if it was happening before my eyes. I would have you understand that I have many enemies in the form of wizards and enchanters, and it is they who have made me act in this way. It is they who persuaded me that this was no play but a real adventure, which cried out for me to take a part in it.

'But I see now,' he went on, 'that I was mistaken. I would not injure this honest showman for the world. Let Master Pedro reckon up everything I owe him, and I will pay him in good Spanish coin before ever I leave this room.'

'Heaven bless your worship!' cried Pedro. 'I could expect no less from such a noble Christian knight. Now let the landlord of this inn and the great Sancho Panza decide how much you must pay.'

Then the showman held up each of the broken puppets in turn and a price was agreed on. First he dis-played the headless body of Marsilius, the Moorish King.

'I don't think I could get a successor to this monarch,' said Master Pedro, 'for less than half a crown. How about half a crown for the King of Saragossa?'

'Agreed,' said Quixote. 'Proceed.'

Next the two halves of the Emperor Charlemagne were held up.

'Truly,' said the showman, 'the Emperor will never be the same again. I think he is worth three and sixpence. I don't see how I can get another Emperor for less.'

'No, no,' said Sancho. 'He's not worth more than half a crown.'

'Let's split the difference,' said the landlord. 'Call it three shillings.'

'No,' interrupted Quixote with some impatience. 'Give him his full price. Don't let's make a fuss about a trifle like sixpence. Give him three and sixpence.'

In this manner a fair price was settled for all the dead and wounded, and Quixote ordered Sancho to pay up in full, with a little extra for the showman's trouble in re-capturing his ape.

'I thank your lordship,' said Master Pedro to Don Quixote, 'for your promptness in settling up so generously.'

'Say no more of that,' answered Quixote. 'But I would give a great deal more to know if Don Gayferos and Melisandra have arrived safely in France, for I never saw them again after the dastardly Moors had begun to pursue them.'

'Well now, that's very easily discovered,' said Master Pedro. 'For who can tell better than my ape? As soon as I find him I'll ask him about our hero and heroine, and I'll let your worship know what he says.'

Then the landlord announced that supper was waiting, and the whole company trooped into the dining-room, where Don Quixote insisted on paying for the whole meal. No one should say that he was not the soul of generosity.

So ended the adventure of the puppet show. After a night's sound sleep Quixote and his squire were up early. Sancho harnessed Rosinante, got ready his ass, and paid the bill. Then knight and squire took their leave and rode out into the morning air.

— 19 —

The Enchanted Bark

For the next two days the weather continued fair and warm, and the knight and his squire were glad to reach a wide river. Here they rode slowly along the grassy bank, enjoying the sight of the broad, smooth water and the green trees at its edge. Don Quixote dreamed lazily of his lady Dulcinea, and Sancho's thoughts travelled to that distant island of which his master had promised to make him governor.

Engaged in these fancies, they soon spied a little boat which lay motionless upon the water, one end moored to the bank by a rope. Don Quixote brought Rosinante to a standstill and looked at it.

'Sancho,' he said at last, 'dismount even as I do, and make fast our steeds to one of these trees that stand by the water's edge.'

So saying, he dismounted, and Sancho did likewise.

185

'What's up now?' asked the squire suspiciously.

'Yonder vessel, if I mistake not,' answered the knight, 'is sent for my especial use. In it I must travel to the spot where some knight is in distress, either imprisoned or facing some implacable foe. Without doubt he has need of my help. When a knight is in distress and no assistance is near, it is usual for some good magician to transport another knight to his aid, either by whirling him through the air or by means of an enchanted bark, such as I perceive this to be.'

'Very well, your worship,' said Sancho, sighing and shrugging his shoulders as he began to tie Rosinante and Dapple to a convenient branch. 'If you ask me, I don't think much of leaving our beasts here to the mercy of magicians and enchanters; but if you say so, I suppose it's all right with me.'

'The same magician who has sent this magic boat,' answered Quixote, 'will undoubtedly protect our steeds from destruction. Make haste, for I am eager to embark.'

'Just as you say, sir. At the same time, I feel it my duty to observe, master, that this here is no enchanted boat, or magic boat, or whatever you call it. This river is pretty well known for the good fishing that's to be had: it's ten to one this is just some fishing boat.'

'Come, let us embark,' said Quixote. 'I think I know an enchanted vessel when I see it—and I think I know my duty too.'

With these words he clambered from the bank on to the boat, and Sancho followed. Then, at his master's bidding, he cut the rope, and the boat began to glide gently down the stream.

When they were in mid-stream, Sancho began quaking with fear, and Dapple's pitiful braying on the bank only added to his distress. Rosinante, too, tried to break loose, and Sancho cried:

'O master, this is indeed a terrible and rash mis-adventure! Hark how my poor donkey calls out at our desertion, and your Rosinante misses you! O miserable animals, I pray Heaven that this prank may end, as usual, in repentance, and my master and I may be brought safely back to the side of our old friends and trusty comrades.'

'Why, what a coward you are!' cried Quixote angrily. 'What a faint-hearted mouse, to be sure! Fancy sitting there trembling all over, while you are carried in state like an arch-duke down this delightful stream, whose placid surface is not disturbed by so much as a ripple. Why, by my reckoning we have travelled seven or eight hundred leagues already, and soon we shall pass out into the great ocean itself, even to the very equator which encircles the centre of the globe.'

'Bless my soul!' cried Sancho. 'Have we got as far as that? I never thought I should live to see the equator. Why did I ever leave my poor wife Teresa and my helpless infants?'

'Aha!' cried Quixote all of a sudden, breaking in upon Sancho's lamentation. 'Do you see yon enchanted castle?'

He pointed down stream to where two great water-mills stood at the edge of the river, their wheels turning slowly in the current.

'Enchanted castle?' cried Sancho. 'Where?'

'Over yonder,' said Quixote. 'Without doubt that is the castle or stronghold in which is confined the knight, or perhaps the queen or princess, whom I am destined to deliver. Now, O my absent lady Dulcinea, star of

Toboso, give me strength to encounter the terrors that await me!'

'That's no fortress, your honour,' said Sancho. 'It's nothing but a couple of water-mills.'

'I grant you, my friend,' answered Quixote, 'that it has the appearance of water-mills. But have you forgotten the strength and cunning of my enemies, the enchanters, in disguising those persons and places I encounter in my exploits? How can you doubt that some wicked enchanter has been at work here?'

'Well, have it your own way,' sighed Sancho, and the boat continued to glide towards the mills.

Soon it was moving more rapidly, and the current carried it towards the mill-wheels. Seeing this, the miller's men came out with their long poles and made ready to push the boat farther out into the stream. Their faces and clothes were all covered with the flour they had been grinding, so that they made a very odd appearance.

'Are you mad?' cried one of the miller's men. 'Get your boat out of the current. You'll smash it to pieces— or else get yourselves knocked to bits by the mill-wheels!'

'Did I not tell you, Sancho,' said Quixote after he had had a good look at the men, 'that we should arrive where I must show my strength and courage? Look what horrid wretches come forth to fight against me! How many hobgoblins stand in my way—look at their deformed faces, their white and ghastly features! You scoundrels,' he continued, addressing the miller's men, 'I'll show you how useless it is to hinder me in the fulfilment of my duty!'

He stood up in the boat and continued to address them in threatening tones.

'You paltry slaves!' he shouted. 'You base and ill-advised scum of the earth! Release instantly the captured knight or dame who is kept a prisoner in your evil fortress, whether they are of high or low degree! I am Don Quixote of la Mancha, otherwise called "the Knight of the Lions", and for my arm is reserved the right and the duty of freeing your prisoner!'

He waved his sword threateningly in the air, while the boat plunged towards the narrow channel in which the mill-wheels were driven round by the force of the current. Sancho was on his knees praying for deliverance, while the men stood on the bank ready to stop the boat with their poles. In this they were successful, but not without letting Quixote and his squire be overturned into the water. Quixote could swim, but the weight of his armour dragged him to the bottom; had it not been for the miller's men, who plunged into the river and dragged them to the bank, knight and squire might both have been drowned. Panting, struggling and drenched to the skin, they floundered ashore. But just then the fishermen to whom the boat belonged, having discovered their loss, had arrived upon the scene.

They found their boat smashed to pieces, and demanded satisfaction of Sancho and his master. Quixote told the fishermen that he would gladly pay for the boat, provided the others would surrender the person who was unjustly imprisoned in their castle.

'What nonsense is this?' said the miller's men. 'What's this castle and this prisoner you're talking about?'

'What's the use of parleying with slaves like these?' said Quixote in despair. 'They understand nothing of chivalry, of prisoners and enchanters. Why, what can I do when there are so many in league against me? One enchanter provides me with a boat, and another undoes his work by overturning it.'

Then the knight planted himself on firm ground under the walls of the mill and cried out in a loud voice:

'O unhappy wretch that is confined within the stones of this hideous fortress, forgive me if I cannot release you at present! All my efforts have been thwarted, and this adventure is reserved for some other knight more fortunate than myself.'

He then ordered Sancho to pay the fishermen for their boat, and this Sancho did with a very ill grace. He hated parting with his master's money, and muttered to himself that if they had any more voyages like that, there would be no money left for food and lodging, and the two of them would certainly starve.

The millers and the fishermen had not the least idea what Quixote was talking about; so, taking him for a madman, they left him and Sancho. The millers went back to their work, and the fishermen made off home, while the knight and the squire, dripping water at every step, took their way slowly back to where their beasts waited anxiously under the trees.

Thus ended the disastrous adventure of the enchanted bark.

Quixote and Sancho wearily remounted their steeds and left the river. Neither the knight nor the squire said anything, but Sancho thought gloomily of the money they had had to pay for the fishing boat.

Next day, towards sunset, they rode out of a wood and found themselves at the edge of a big meadow, at the other end of which was a group of people. Quixote saw that they were persons of quality engaged in the pastime of hawking. One of the ladies had a goshawk upon her wrist and rode on a fine white horse.

'Sancho,' said the knight, calling to his squire, 'run and tell that lady on the palfrey that I, the Knight of the Lions, humbly salute her highness and, if she pleases to give me leave, I shall be proud to have the honour of waiting on her and kissing her fair hand.'

Sancho did as he was told and, forcing Dapple to something like a gallop, came within a few paces of the fair lady. He dismounted and fell on one knee before her.

'Fair lady,' said he, 'that knight yonder, called the Knight of the Lions, is my master. I am his squire, Sancho Panza by name. I am sent to pay you my master's humble respects and to say that, if you will graciously deign to receive him, he will be proud to become your high and mightiness' eternal slave—or something of the sort.'

'Well spoken, sir,' answered the lady, bestowing on Sancho a charming smile. 'Rise, I beg you, for it is not fitting that the squire to so noble a knight should kneel. Pray tell your master that if he will be pleased to accept of our hospitality, my lord Duke and I will gladly entertain him at our house, which is not far off. We have heard of the exploits of the Knight of the Lions, you may be sure.'

Sancho, highly delighted with this answer, scrambled on to the ass's back once more and returned to his master's side.

'O sir,' he exclaimed, 'she's a wonder, that duchess. She isn't half a good looker, sir, if you ask me. You come and see for yourself. She and her old man want us to go and visit them in their castle. They know about us too—they've heard about our adventures.'

At this Don Quixote sat upright in his saddle and arranged his visor in what he thought was a becoming angle. He and Sancho then made their way across the meadow to where the Duke and the Duchess were awaiting them. Sancho prepared to leap to the ground and hold Quixote's stirrup for him to dismount gracefully. But as ill luck would have it, his foot caught in the rope that secured his stirrup to the saddle, and he fell sideways, where he hung, head downwards, unable to free his foot. Quixote meanwhile was obliged to dismount without assistance and, his saddle being badly fastened, it slipped to the ground with the knight upon it. So, while Sancho hung helpless from his ass, Quixote sprawled on the ground, unable to move because of the weight of his armour.

The Duke graciously sent some of his followers to assist the knight and the squire. Apologies having been made for the clumsiness of their approach, and compliments being exchanged on both sides, the party set off towards the Duke's castle which, as the lady had said, was not far distant.

Here Don Quixote was sumptuously entertained for so long as he wished to stay. The Duke and his lady were extremely pleasant and lively companions. They had heard of the fame of Don Quixote, and were delighted to entertain in their own home the man who had performed so many noteworthy feats of arms. He and the knight talked much of knight errantry, while the Duchess was equally delighted with the simple humour and country ways of the honest squire.

'But how about Sancho Panza's island?' asked the Duke one evening, when Sancho was out in the stables,

193

seeing to the welfare of Rosinante and Dapple. 'Do you not think, sir knight, that he should at last be rewarded for his services in the manner you have promised?'

'I do indeed, your grace,' answered Quixote, 'but so far no convenient island has fallen into my hands, so that I cannot as yet reward him with a governorship.'

'I have an idea,' continued the Duke. 'Let us make him governor of a small town that lies within my estates. We will tell him that, while it is not exactly an island, he can look upon it as such during the term of his office. It is called Barataria, and it has about a thousand inhabitants. I will arrange for my steward to look after him, and I will see that the principal citizens of the town are warned in advance to treat him as their governor, and to allow him to rule them. The Duchess and I, you may be sure, will be heartily pleased to hear reports of his governorship.'

'I'm afraid,' said Quixote, 'that poor Sancho will make a sorry mess of the business. He is but a simple peasant and not used to a position of authority.'

'Nevertheless, sir knight,' put in the Duchess, 'we insist on trying this experiment. It will be highly diverting, and after all, it is only fair that Sancho's longing for power should be satisfied. Here we have the means to do it, so let us make arrangements at once.'

So it was agreed. Sancho was informed, to his intense delight, that he had been appointed governor of a small island or township in the Duke's domains, called Barataria, and that he was to take up his appointment at once.

Sancho was overjoyed to hear of his good fortune. He resolved to have a letter sent to his wife Teresa to inform her of the honour that had been paid to him. The Duke's steward was given the task of seeing to Sancho's needs and of acquainting him with the duties of a town governor.

'At first, you know,' said Sancho to his master, 'I shan't know what to do. Still, I'll manage all right. I've got a few ideas of how a place should be run.'

Don Quixote devoted considerable trouble to instructing his squire in the management of an island. He told him how he would have to receive important visitors in audience, attend state functions, and settle disputes between his subjects.

At last the moment approached when Sancho was to set out for his island, as it was called. He was given a mule to ride, and he was dressed in a silk robe with a cap to match. Dapple followed behind, laden with rich trappings like a horse of state; this so delighted Sancho that he kept turning round throughout the journey to observe his ass so gorgeously bedecked. Behind the ass rode the Duke's steward and numerous other servants who had been appointed to wait upon the new governor of Barataria. When the moment came for departing, Sancho kissed the hands of the Duke and Duchess and received the blessing of his master. Quixote's eyes were filled with tears at parting with his faithful squire; as for Sancho, proud though he was of the great honour which had befallen him, he blubbered like a child leaving home for the first time. But everyone wished him joy and good fortune, so that it was with very mixed feelings that he rode forth at the head of his train to fulfil the ambition of his life.

— 20 —

Governor Sancho

When Sancho and his train reached the town, the bells were rung and the principal officers came out to meet him, dressed in their ceremonial robes. The people were almost mad with joy, dancing and singing in the streets, clapping their hands and shouting salutations. The dogs barked, the little boys fought, and the stall-keepers in the market shut up their stalls for the day and joined in the festivities. Amidst these universal rejoicings, Sancho was led in state to the great church to give thanks to Heaven for his preservation. He was then formally presented with the keys of the town gates and proclaimed sole ruler of the island of Barataria.

Sancho's plain country appearance and his short stout figure made a good many people wonder about the quality of their new governor, and even those who knew all about the jest were doubtful as to how it would turn out.

196

But there was hearty cheering as Sancho was carried from the church to the court of justice, where he was set up on a throne at one end of the great hall. There he sat looking at the throng of people in front of him; then, turning round, he noticed an inscription on the wall above his head. It recorded the history of the town and paid some flowery compliments to the ancestors of the Duke in whose lands the town was situated. But as Sancho could not read, he asked the steward what the inscription meant.

'Sir governor,' answered the steward, 'it commemorates the day on which your lordship was appointed governor of this island and concludes with the words "LONG LIVE SEÑOR DON SANCHO PANZA, ILLUSTRIOUS GOVERNOR OF THE ISLE OF BARATARIA". I trust you are not displeased.'

'Who is this Señor Don Sancho Panza?' asked Sancho. 'It can't be me.'

'Indeed it is, sire,' answered the steward. 'Who else could it be? There are no Panzas besides yourself in Barataria.'

'I'm no Don,' objected Sancho. 'My grandfather was plain Sancho, my father was Sancho, and all of us are just Panza, with none of your Señors and Dons. Just you remember that, young fellow. I'll tell you what— there's probably too many Dons altogether in this island, and if I have my way, one of the first things I'll do is to get rid of a few of them!'

This speech was received with general approval, and a murmur of applause broke out from those near enough to Sancho to hear what he said. Those who could not hear leaned forward and asked others to repeat his words.

'What's that he said?' asked one old citizen of his neighbour.

'He said there were too many lords and gentlemen in the town.'

'Quite right too,' agreed the other. 'First bit of sense I've heard in this hall for twenty years.'

'That's so,' said the other. 'This fellow may not be much to look at, but he has a bit of sense in that head of his. Let's hear what else he has to say.'

The steward thought it wisest to change the subject.

'Now sire,' he continued, 'it is the custom here for the governor to settle all disputes arising between his subjects, so that the people may see whether they have got a wise or an unwise ruler. Will your majesty condescend to listen to these men?'

Two men had come to the court for judgment. One was a tailor and the other a farmer. The farmer had come to the tailor's shop with a piece of cloth, asking if it was big enough to make a cap.

'Why, certainly,' the tailor had said.

But the farmer had feared the tailor meant to cheat him out of part of his cloth, so he had asked if it would make two.

'Yes, I think so,' the tailor had told him.

'In that case,' went on the farmer, 'perhaps it will make three.'

In the end the tailor had undertaken to make as many as five caps from the farmer's piece of cloth. But when he had shown him the caps, the farmer had refused to pay.

'Not a penny can I get out of him,' complained the tailor, 'though I have made the five caps as agreed, and never an inch of his cloth have I taken for myself.'

'Can you produce the caps in this court?' asked Sancho.

'Yes, indeed, your majesty,' the tailor replied; and pulling his hand out from under his coat, he displayed five tiny caps, each one perched on a finger or a thumb. At this everyone laughed except Sancho, who sat gravely considering the matter. At last he spoke.

'I don't think this case need keep us long,' he said, 'for it can be settled very easily. You, master tailor, shall lose your labour, and you, master farmer, your cloth. It is my judgment that these caps shall be given to the poor of the town for their children to play with. They will make excellent headwear for dolls. See that my judgment is carried out.'

At this there was general laughter and applause. Undoubtedly the new governor was a wise man.

Next came two old men, one of whom complained that a long time ago he had lent the other old man ten gold crowns which had never been repaid.

'Your majesty,' said the old man who had lent the money, and who was called Juan, 'he borrowed the ten crowns from me in time of need, and I did not press him for a long time. But now I am forced to ask for my money, and he says he repaid me some months ago. We have no witnesses, so I have brought him before this court. If he will swear upon his honour as a Christian gentleman that he repaid me, I have no more to say.'

'What say you to this?' asked Sancho of the other old man, whose name was Carlos, and who supported himself with a thick cane staff.

'I paid him back his ten crowns,' said Carlos. 'He's an old man, your majesty, and he's forgotten.'

'Will you swear this upon my rod of justice?' asked Sancho.

'Certainly,' answered Carlos. 'Here,' he continued,

addressing Juan, 'hold my cane for me while I take the rod of justice.'

So saying, he handed Juan his cane and took Sancho's rod.

'Now then,' he said, 'as I am a Christian gentleman, I swear upon this rod that I have given into the hands of Master Juan the ten gold pieces he lent me.'

He then handed back Sancho's rod and took back his cane from the other old man.

'What do you say to this?' asked Sancho of Juan. 'Are you satisfied?'

'I am indeed,' said Juan. 'I own that I must have forgotten my debt was repaid.'

'I thank your majesty,' said Carlos, and with a low bow before Sancho he began to walk down the hall, supported by his cane.

'One moment,' called Sancho after him. 'Come back, old man. Let me have a look at that cane of yours.'

Carlos did as he was bidden, and Sancho took the cane and handed it to Juan.

'There,' he said, 'in case you are not fully satisfied let this cane repay your debt.'

'How's this?' said Juan in surprise. 'He owed me ten gold crowns, and your majesty repays me with a cane.'

Sancho turned to one of the court officers.

'Let the cane be broken,' he ordered.

The official did as he was told, and when the hollow cane was broken, out rolled ten gold pieces on to the floor of the hall. Juan picked them up in astonishment and joy, while Carlos left the court in disgrace. Everyone cheered Sancho loudly, and someone asked him how he had guessed that the money was inside the cane.

'Why,' said Sancho, 'I saw that this old man, Master

Juan, was a patient and honest-looking fellow; and when the other gave him his staff to hold and then swore that he had handed the money over to Master Juan, I at once saw the trick. And now,' he concluded, 'I hope you consider I've got enough sense to make a good governor.'

The steward and the officials agreed heartily, and Sancho was then led from the hall of justice to a banqueting room, where a great table was spread with magnificent dishes and glass and cutlery of the finest. Four pages stood ready to attend him, and music played while he washed his hands. By now Sancho was thoroughly hungry, so he prepared to set to with a will. Then a gentleman who afterwards turned out to be a doctor waved a white wand of office over the table, and one of the pages removed a fine cloth which covered the dishes. Sancho took his place at the head of the table on the only seat provided, for he was to dine in state with no others sitting down beside him. Then one of the serving men placed a dish of fruit before him. Sancho's mouth watered in anticipation, and he was about to take a bunch of choice grapes when the doctor waved his wand, and a page removed the fruit.

Next a dish of meat was set before him, and once more Sancho prepared to eat. But once more the doctor waved his wand, and the dish was whisked away in an instant.

'Is it your custom here,' asked Sancho, 'to tantalize your guests with the sight and smell of food which they aren't allowed to taste? Funny sort of custom, if you ask me.'

'My lord governor,' said the doctor, 'I am Doctor Rezio, and it is my business to supervise the health of your lordship. My first duty is to attend you at table and see that you do not eat what may be harmful to you. Now that fruit is far too moist and soft to do you any good, and I have therefore banished it from your table. That dish of meat was too hot and spicy, and could have done you no good at all.'

'I see,' said Sancho, highly disappointed. 'Then this dish of partridges, which I see a serving man has set before me, would be just right, eh?'

'By no means!' cried Doctor Rezio, waving his wand. 'Take it away instantly, page. It is the very worst thing for your lordship's constitution.'

'Doctor Rezio,' said Sancho, 'please stop telling me what I may not eat, and proceed to tell me what I may.'

'Well,' continued the doctor, 'that veal over there might have been all right if it had not been roast, but that rabbit is no good at all. I fear there is nothing here that is suitable for your consumption, so——'

'Look here, Master Doctor,' cried Sancho, rising from his chair in anger, 'just you get out of here and leave me to eat in peace! Otherwise I go home at once, and you can keep your island! A governorship which doesn't give the governor the chance of a square meal isn't worth two beans. Get out of here, or I'll brush your hair with the legs of my chair, do you hear?'

Doctor Rezio in alarm was just going to flee from the hall when the sound of a post-horn was heard.

A messenger entered hurriedly with an urgent letter for Sancho.

'It is from the Duke,' he said, 'and concerns your ear alone.'

Everyone was sent out of the room except the steward and Sancho's secretary, who proceeded to read as follows:

'To Don Sancho Panza, governor of the isle of Barataria, greetings!

'It has come to my knowledge that our enemies are likely to make a surprise attack upon the island. Some spies are already reported to have secretly entered the city, where they await an opportunity to kill your honour. Be careful whom you admit to your presence, and eat nothing that is set before you. I will send help when necessary. Look to your safety, and be of good courage.

'Your friend the DUKE.'

At this Sancho was astonished, and turning to the secretary, he said:

'Write me a letter at once and send it to the Duke. Tell him I will do as he says. Ask him to give my compliments to my lady the Duchess and remind her to send a letter to my wife Teresa to say how I am getting on. Give my respects also to my master Don Quixote, so that he may know I don't forget him.'

Then turning to the steward, Sancho continued:

'Have that Doctor Rezio clapped into prison at once.

I'm sure he is one of my enemies and is out to kill me by the worst possible death—starvation.'

'Nevertheless, your highness,' said the steward, 'it would perhaps be unwise to eat any of the things on this table. You can't tell but what they are poisoned.'

'True,' said Sancho, 'but a man must eat something. If we are going to have fighting, we can't do that on empty stomachs! Get me some bread and four pounds of raisins—there can't be anything wrong with that, and it'll keep me going for the time being.'

In the end Sancho had nothing to eat till supper time, but he was well satisfied with that. Everyone spoke well of his wisdom and shrewdness as governor; and the Duke, the Duchess and Don Quixote, when they heard reports of him, were highly delighted.

Accordingly the Duchess sent a page to Sancho's home in la Mancha with a letter which Sancho had got his secretary to write to his wife Teresa. She also sent a coral necklace of her own as a present. When the page arrived at the home of Sancho Panza, he bowed low before Teresa and said:

'I have the honour to greet the lady Donna Teresa Panza, wife of the governor of the island of Barataria!'

'What's all this?' asked Teresa in bewilderment, wiping her hands on her apron. 'I'm no Donna Teresa, but plain Teresa Panza. Do not make fun of me, sir, I beg.'

'By no means,' answered the page. 'If madam will but read the letter I have brought from the governor, and receive the present which he has sent, she will understand everything.'

Both Teresa and her daughter Sanchica, who was with her when the page arrived, were amazed at this news;

and Teresa asked the page to read her husband's letter, for she could not herself read a word. With the deepest interest they listened to the description of how Sancho had been made governor over a thousand people, and how his wisdom had won him a great reputation, and how the Duke and the Duchess were full of admiration for him.

'And the Duchess has sent this necklace of coral and gold all for me!' cried Teresa. 'Fancy that.'

'It's long enough to be made into two, mother,' said Sanchica; 'then there'll be one for me.'

They ran and told the priest and the barber and Samson Carrasco, and they were all equally amazed and gratified to hear of Sancho's good fortune. There was great rejoicing in the village, and everyone talked about the hero Don Sancho Panza, who had been made ruler of an island by a great Duke.

Meanwhile, Sancho continued to govern with great success, making a number of laws and altering regulations whenever he thought them unjust. He altered the prices of all sorts of goods and put men's wages up or down whenever they struck him as too low or too high. The only complaint he had was that he himself was never allowed enough to eat. So far he had heard nothing more of the plot to kill him, but when he had been governor for a week, those who had carried on the jest felt it was time to bring it to an end.

One night, when Sancho was trying to get some sleep after a toilsome day of giving judgments and passing laws, he was awakened by a terrible noise of drums and trumpets, which was accompanied by the ringing of all the bells in the city. He started up in a terrible fright. In night-shirt and slippers he ran out into the corridor, where a number of men carrying torches had come to give the alarm.

'Rise up, my lord governor!' they cried. 'Arm yourself and be prepared for the worst! A world of enemies have got into the island, and we are lost unless your valour can save us!'

'I know nothing of arms,' said poor Sancho, his teeth chattering with fright. 'Send for my master, Don Quixote. He'll settle your enemies for you.'

'For shame, my lord governor,' said one of the men. 'See, I bring you arms both offensive and defensive. Lead the ranks of your loyal subjects to the market-place, and show yourself our captain!'

'V-v-very w-well then,' said Sancho. 'Arm me, and may Heaven p-preserve me!'

Without waiting for him to put on his clothes, they fitted two shields over his night-shirt, one in front and the other behind. These were strapped tightly to his body, so that Sancho was unable to bend his knees or stir a step in any direction. They then put a lance into his hand for him to use as a staff, and told him to march forth and lead them on.

'March?' said Sancho. 'How do you expect me to do that, wedged as I am between these shields? You'll have to carry me to some important spot and stand me up— and then I'll fight as well as I can with my lance.'

'Fie, my lord!' said another of the men. 'You *must* march. That is the duty of our leader.'

They pushed him forward, so that poor Sancho was obliged to make an effort to move, whereupon he fell flat on his face like a tortoise or an upturned boat. Then the men, far from having any mercy on him and helping him to rise, put out their lights so that he could not see

what was happening. Then they shouted and screamed,
clashed their swords together, jumped up and down, and
made as much noise as if they had been really engaged
with the enemy. Sancho, if he had not kept his head
firmly between the shields, would certainly have been
trampled to death. Even so, the men tumbled over him
and jumped upon him, while he lay all the while fixed
firmly between the shields, sweating with fear and vowing
never to have anything more to do with the business of
governing islands.

Someone stood upon Sancho's body and called out
imaginary commands, such as 'Charge, boys!' 'The
enemy is coming up in the rear.' 'Guard that gate!'
'Fetch fire-balls—bring more grenades—send for burning
pitch and boiling oil!' 'Barricade the streets!'

'O lord,' Sancho prayed fervently, 'send a speedy end
to this battle. If you will not grant peace, grant me
death!'

Then he heard the men cry, 'Victory, victory! The
enemy is beaten! See how they fly. Now, my lord governor,
rise! Come forth and enjoy the fruits of conquest. Let us
divide the spoils taken from the enemy by the strength of
your unconquerable arms!'

They helped Sancho to his feet and unstrapped the
shields. A pitiful sight he looked, all bruised and shaking.

'You can keep the spoils of victory,' said he. 'All I
want is a cup of wine to quench my thirst.'

They gave him wine, and presently Sancho, overcome
with fatigue and the shock of the imaginary battle,
fainted away on his bed. They began to think they had
taken the joke too far, but Sancho soon recovered and
asked what time it was.

They told him it was near break of day, and without

another word he began to put on his clothes. All the while he was silent, the eyes of his companions were fixed on him. Then he rose stiffly from the bed and hobbled out of the room. They followed him to the stable, where he found Dapple and began embracing the creature with tears in his eyes.

'Ah, faithful friend,' he said, 'sharer of my misfortunes and companion in my travels, why did I forsake you? Since I left you to climb the ladder of ambition, a thousand cares, a thousand torments, and four thousand woes have fallen upon me.'

He fitted the saddle on to the ass, while everyone watched to see what he would do. Without another word he slowly mounted into the saddle. Then turning to the steward, the secretary, Doctor Rezio and all the other servants and officials, he said:

'Make way, gentlemen, and let me return to my former liberty. I intend to go back home and begin again the life I left. I was not born to govern kingdoms, to overthrow enemies, to make laws and pass judgment. I know more of ploughing, and digging, and planting, and caring for vineyards. I'd rather have a spade in my hand than a governor's staff, and I'd rather fill my belly with plain honest food than be at the mercy of a crafty doctor who starves me to death. Every man to his trade, say I. Let the carpenter stick to his saw, and the shoemaker to his last. Tell my lord Duke that my governorship is at an end, and that I take no more out of his island than I brought into it. I would rather cover my body with coarse homespun than spend sleepless nights between the linen sheets of slavery. Stand aside then, gentlemen. My enemies have walked over me all night, and I believe all my ribs are broken. I will therefore get me home as fast as I conveniently can, and find relief for my injuries.'

'My lord governor,' said Doctor Rezio, 'allow me to provide you with a certain balsam whereof I know the secret, which shall heal all your hurts and render you proof against further discomfort. As for your diet, I will in future regulate it so that you may enjoy a little more of the food and drink suitable to a man of your lordship's rank.'

'No,' said Sancho firmly. 'I am not to be caught twice by the same trick, Master Doctor. Keep your balsam, for I don't need it. Nor do I need any more of your delicious disappearing dishes, for I am going where I shall get plainer fare.'

Next the steward tried to persuade him to stay, but Sancho refused. Everyone applauded his good sense and Christian forgiveness. Then the steward asked him if there was anything he would like, and he asked for only a bag of oats for his donkey, and a loaf of bread and some cheese for himself. When these had been brought, he bade farewell to them all, not without tears in his eyes, and urged Dapple gently forward. They saw him to the gates, and presently he was out of the town, or island, of Barataria, which he wished never more to behold. So ended the short but memorable governorship of the wise and honest Señor Don Sancho Panza.

— 21 —

The Last Adventure

When Sancho got back to the Duke's castle, he was welcomed by everyone and complimented on his successful governorship; but he told them he had a mind to go home and see his wife Teresa, his daughter Sanchica, and his other children. Don Quixote himself was beginning to think it was time for him to end his pleasant stay at the castle and once more take the road in search of adventure. Both knight and squire, therefore, were preparing to depart when there appeared a stranger at the castle.

Don Quixote happened to be exercising in a meadow, fully armed, when he heard a voice behind him. Turning, he saw another knight, armed like himself and on horseback, advancing towards him. The stranger addressed him in an elevated tone of voice.

'Illustrious and never-to-be-sufficiently-extolled Don Quixote of la Mancha,' said he, 'I am the Knight of the

211

White Moon, of whose unspeakable valour you have no doubt heard.'

Don Quixote looked at the knight and saw that he did indeed bear a shield on which was portrayed a crescent moon in shining silver. He was about to reply when the knight continued:

'I am come to engage in combat with you and test your skill and strength. I intend to make you confess that my mistress, whoever she may be, is incomparably more lovely and gracious than your lady Dulcinea of Toboso.'

'Sir knight, whoever you are,' answered Quixote, 'I shall do no such thing!'

'If you freely confess this truth,' the Knight of the White Moon continued, ignoring Quixote's protest, 'you will spare your own life and save me the trouble of taking it. The conditions of the combat are these: if you lose, you shall not only confess the superiority of my lady over yours, but you shall also return to your own dwelling and lay down your arms for the space of a year, promising to give up the practice of knight errantry for the whole of that time. If, on the other hand, you shall prove the victor, my horse and arms will be at your disposal, and the fame of my exploits shall be transferred to you, exactly as if you had performed them yourself. Make haste and decide whether or not to accept my challenge, for this very day shall determine the dispute between us.'

Don Quixote was amazed at the arrogance and presumption of the Knight of the White Moon, but, controlling his anger, he answered with dignity:

'Sir knight, whoever you are, I am convinced that you have never had the good fortune to behold the lady Dulcinea of Toboso; otherwise you would not presume to make comparison between her beauty and that of any

other lady on earth. However, I am content to accept
your challenge upon the conditions you mention—with
one exception. If I am victorious, I have no desire that
the fame of your exploits shall be transferred to me. I
have never heard of you, and have no knowledge whatever of your exploits. I shall therefore remain content
with my own. Now sir, choose your ground, for I am
ready to engage in battle with you as, when and where you
please!'

The Duke, who had been informed of the arrival of
the Knight of the White Moon, hastened out of his
castle to see what was afoot. He arrived with the Duchess,
his steward, and a number of other followers just as
Quixote had turned Rosinante about, in order to make
his career. The Duke rode up to the strange knight and
asked him the reason of the combat. The knight explained
the matter to the Duke, who rode a little distance off and
asked his steward who the stranger might be.

'I haven't the least idea, your highness,' answered the
steward. 'But I dare say this is only some new jest. Let us
see what happens.'

So everyone looked on, half in curiosity and half in
amusement, while Quixote and his adversary once more
turned their horses about and prepared to charge. Without any signal from trumpet or herald, they brought
their horses face to face with each other at the same
moment. Each clapped spurs to the sides of his mount, and
instantly that belonging to the Knight of the White Moon,
being a swift and agile beast, sprang forward. Rosinante,
on the other hand, having no mind for the fray, bestirred
himself without haste, so that Quixote's adversary was
upon him before he had finished commending himself
to God and the lady Dulcinea. So impetuously did the

Knight of the White Moon charge upon him that both horse and rider were flung violently to the ground, where they lay sprawling and helpless. The victor instantly sprang from his steed and held the point of his lance to Quixote's face.

'Señor Don Quixote,' he cried, 'you are vanquished and a dead man unless you confess according to the conditions of our combat!'

Don Quixote, without stirring, groaned feebly and said in a voice which might have come from the grave:

'The lady Dulcinea of Toboso is the most beautiful person on earth. Sir knight, I am at your mercy. Since you have taken my honour, take my life also. Strike home and spare not!'

'Not so,' said the Knight of the White Moon chivalrously. 'Long may the fame and beauty of the lady Dulcinea be confessed. All I demand is that you submit to one year's retirement at home, and give up all exercise of arms for that period.'

Don Quixote, gratified at the chivalry of his conqueror, readily promised to abide by this condition. His honour was preserved, and he solemnly promised to go home and give up knight errantry for a year. The Duke, the Duchess, and all present having heard his promise, Quixote was helped to his feet; the Knight of the White Moon made a solemn bow to the whole company, and without further speech remounted, clapped spurs to his horse, and galloped away towards the town.

The Duke sent his steward after him to inquire who he was, for his curiosity was aroused by the mysterious knight who had conquered Don Quixote. Meanwhile, when Quixote's helmet was removed, they found the poor knight pale and dejected. Rosinante too was bruised and stunned by his fall; so that both horse and rider were in sorry condition. Sancho, who had looked on with dismay in his heart, at first thought he was dreaming, or that the whole adventure had been brought about by enchantment. He seemed to see his master stripped of all his glory, utterly downcast and looking as if he would die.

'O my poor master,' he murmured, 'how have you been overcome? Of what use now is the pride and strength which made you victor over the windmills, the giant Mambrino and those fearsome lions? How will you ever hold up your head again?'

Slowly and sorrowfully Quixote was helped back to the castle, where for six days he remained in bed to recover his strength after the bruises and shaking he had received from his fall.

The steward, meanwhile, had pursued the Knight of the White Moon to an inn in the town, where he found the stranger engaged in removing his armour.

'Tell me,' he said, 'now we are alone, who you are, and why you sought out poor old Don Quixote and knocked him off his horse.'

'There's no need for concealment, I suppose,' answered the stranger. 'My name is Samson Carrasco, and I come from the village in la Mancha where Quixote lives. Everyone there thinks he is out of his mind, and that the only way to cure him is to get him to give up knight errantry. Some time ago I rode out disguised as the Knight of the Mirrors, but he beat me in fair fight and I wasn't able to make him give up his madness. But this time it's different. As you saw for yourself, I've at last made him promise to stay quietly at home and stop making a fool of himself. There's no chance of his breaking his word, so let's hope he's finally cured this time.'

'H'm,' answered the steward, 'perhaps you're right. But if you ask me, it's a great pity. He's given us all plenty of sport. Still, I dare say you know best.'

'Without doubt,' answered Samson. 'Keep my secret, I beg you, and don't let on that it was I who conquered him, and not the illustrious and never-to-be-forgotten Knight of the White Moon.'

The steward promised he would say nothing to Quixote and took his leave. Then he returned to the Duke and told him what he had discovered. The Duke and Duchess were both sorry to see the last of their amusing guest—not to mention his honest squire Sancho, who had given them such pleasure and entertainment.

The knight was sunk in melancholy as they jogged slowly back towards la Mancha. Sancho did his best to cheer him up.

'Don't be so miserable, sir,' he said. 'Remember,

whatever happened at the castle, you're still the Knight of the Lions. It's a long lane that has no turning, sir, and every cloud has a silver lining. Think of what *I've* lost! I didn't much care for being governor, it's true; but I wasn't half looking forward to being a duke or an earl. But now I'll have to forget about all that and go back to looking after pigs.'

'I shall never give up my profession,' answered Quixote. 'This retirement is only for a year. Once that time has passed, I shall take up again my title and my arms, and the world shall re-echo with the fame of my deeds. After such adventures as ours, Sancho, what else have I to live for?'

'Well, we'll see about that, your honour,' said Sancho. 'Don't count your chickens before they're hatched—that's what I say. Let's go home and dream about all the wonderful things we've done together. Oh, I shall never forget those fulling-mills, sir, and how brave you were, tackling them all by yourself!'

So they rode on, knight and squire, horse and ass, till at length they came, towards evening, within sight of their own village.

The priest and Samson Carrasco were walking in the fields when Quixote and Sancho rode up. They hastened to greet them, and were overjoyed at their return. Together they went up to Quixote's house, where the housekeeper and the niece ran out to meet them. A boy had seen them as they went through the village, and had hastened to Sancho's home to tell Teresa of her husband's return. Hand in hand with Sanchica, she hurried through the village to Quixote's house, where Sanchica threw her arms round her father and asked what he had brought for her.

217

'It seems to me, husband,' said Teresa, 'that you don't look much like the governor of an island. Where are your robes of office and your trumpeter?'

'Peace, wife,' said Sancho. 'There's many a slip 'twixt the cup and the lip. But let us go home together, and I'll tell you all about it.'

So taking leave of his master, Sancho walked home with his wife and daughter, leading the patient Dapple by the halter. They spent the evening talking and laughing over all that had passed, and Sancho vowed that, even if Teresa were no longer the wife of the governor of an island, one day he would make her a princess or an earl's wife at the least.

'That's as may be,' answered Teresa. 'But until that time comes, you just stay with me and earn an honest living.'

Don Quixote was by no means so confident of taking up his adventures again. For a time he was ill and stayed in bed, but on his recovery he told the priest and the barber and Samson Carrasco all about his defeat and how he had sworn to remain at home in retirement for a year.

'Well,' said Samson gaily, 'a year will soon pass. Then you can be off again and perform even greater exploits than before in the service of the peerless Dulcinea.'

'No,' said Quixote, 'I may never go wandering again. I have been thinking while I have been in bed, and it seems to me that I've committed many follies in my time, and now I should bethink me of returning to ym right mind. Those books of mine have led me into much madness, so that I've been a cause of anxiety and sorrow to those who love me best. Give me a year to think it over—then perhaps I shall have come to my senses.'

At this Quixote's friends murmured in sympathy and

approval, and his niece and his housekeeper went to the kitchen to prepare food for them all. Presently the meal was ready, and there we must leave them. Everyone was relieved that Quixote had once more resolved to live like a simple country gentleman. He became quiet and thoughtful, though he no longer looked melancholy. His cheek was as sunken and his brow as careworn as ever, but he appeared like a man who has undergone great trials and seen brave adventures. Perhaps he was thinking of the days long ago—the days when knights on horseback, in shining armour, rode about the world slaying dragons, rescuing maidens in distress, and challenging each other to mortal combat.

As for Rosinante, he munched his oats contentedly in the stable; and what went on in his old head, with its two sad eyes, no one can tell.